Candy Rain,
Candy Kisses

Candy Rain,
Candy Kisses

CLEOTILDE

Order this book online at www.trafford.com
or email orders@trafford.com

Most Trafford titles are also available at major online book retailers.

Printed in the United States of America.

ISBN: 978-1-4669-2024-8 (sc)

Trafford rev. 03/23/2012

 www.trafford.com

North America & international
toll-free: 1 888 232 4444 (USA & Canada)
phone: 250 383 6864 ♦ fax: 812 355 4082

Dedicated to Mom and Dad

Chapter 1

I t was a cold November day in New York City, a Wednesday to be exact, and Claudia had more than she could handle that day at work. Working in a fashion industry the stress could be over whelming and listening to all the fuss and all of what people with no fashion sense, thought was a fashion statement, was all that she could handle for the day.

Claudia was a fashion designer and worked in uptown Manhattan, even though she was a small town designer venturing out to the big apple, it was a successful job that she loved and took very seriously, so serious that her career pretty much took over her social life, not much of one considering she lived in the big apple, but for Claudia it was a fulfilling life, one that she worked hard to have, it kept her feed and living nicely, so what more could a girl ask for . . . .

Claudia, almost 40, stood 5'2", long dark brown hair, beautiful full lips, not fat but not thin, very curvacious, thick, what most Texans would say, and had a personality that would melt your heart. Claudia loved being around people, and she always had so much to say, a Texas girl with Texan values, she was a comedian without even realizing or trying to be one, she was just one of those persons that you loved being around. Even though Claudia didn't have a social life she would go have a drink or two, she would take time from her busy schedule and hang out at one of the many pubs that New York had to offer, it wasn't often but it was enough to let out the stress when she needed it. Now Claudia didn't know to many people since she only resided there 18 months come January, but there was one person that she became familiar with and was like family, Lola.

Now Lola was a widowed 43 year old who worked in the same building as Claudia (that's how they met) as a make up artist for people in commercials, she also had her hands showcased in a couple of commercials for dish-washing liquid, something she was very proud of and bragged about from time to time. She worked long hours and really didn't like to go out as much, but in essence would attempt it, she would have a drink or two with Claudia just to keep her company in the big apple.

Claudia and Lola had a nice, close, friendship, if you didn't know them you would think they were sisters that's how they treated each other, close sisters. Claudia was the social one and Lola kinda of was a kickback kind of person. She liked to sit back and scope out the scene, before you knew it she could tell you everything that went on that night with everyone around them, she herself could be a comedian without even realizing it. Well it was a hectic Wednesday and Claudia and Lola decided to hang out that evening, since it was the big apple it didn't matter what day of the week you went out something was always happening. Claudia was feeling the Cosmos (a popular martini that Claudia loved) so they decided to have a couple of drinks at a popular hang out called Lu Lu's, not your typical New York type of hang out but it was around the corner from were Claudia lived and Lola didn't live to far so it was a mutual hang out were both of them could let loose and make it home safe.

They both walked in and to the right was one of the guys that worked in the shipping department next to their building, Hank, a tall, bald, cocky son of a gun, that neither one of them really liked but after a couple of drinks, loosened up and was acceptable for the night, so they darted off across the bar to say hello and play a couple of games of pool. Claudia ordered her cosmo and Lola ordered her tequila as they sat there conversing, waiting for the alcohol to kick in on Hank, a tall slender light complected, dark haired guy walked in, his sense of confidence as he walked, caught Claudia's eye. She sat there and continued to carry her conversation with Hank noticing that this tall slender man was heading there direction, he extended his hand to give a firm handshake to Hank staring right at Claudia, Hank continued to introduce him to the girls, his name was Craig, he had worked with Hank, 2 years ago, in another shipping department. Hank, being as cocky as he was, introducing the girls as his playmates, with no laughter coming from neither one of them they continued to introduce themselves, Claudia's eyes locked with his, there was something about him that caught her attention and she wanted badly to find out what it was.

Craig sat there quiet with not much to say but his body language had a whole different vibe that Claudia could feel through her body. His lips were full and she could imagine hers pressed up against his running her tongue around his lips locking them together softly touching, she imagined them tasting like candy kisses. After a few moments of awkward silence his lips broke apart to speak to her and ask her if she didn't mind but how old she was. Claudia hesitated, wondering if this was a insult waiting to happen, she paused took a deep breath and answered with "almost 40". Craig stood there with a look of she didn't know what, with a tiny grin his response was sweet, "You couldn't possibly be 40, I thought you where in your late 20's!" Feeling a rush of heat through her face, she asked the same question, his answer threw her back, he was 23 . . . .

After what seemed to be a eternity but was actually only 10 minutes, Hank made his way back to Craig and Claudia, drunk and ready to leave Hank said his goodbyes with Craig following right behind him. Lola a bit tipsy herself, was ready to inform Claudia of all the gossip around the bar that she picked up on that night, with Craig on her mind Lola's voice seemed like muffled noise and nothing she said made sense, all Claudia could think of was Craig and if she'd ever see him again.

The next day Claudia had a big order to fill, she designed a halter top for plus sized women that curved out the waist and gave a illusion of a slender upper body sized, it was popular in Texas and orders were being filled quicker than they were being made, it was her biggest accomplishment yet. With all the excitement of this order she had no time to think of Craig but as the night settled in and the last shipment was being loaded to the trucks he popped into her head. Was she reading him right? Was he interested in her, a 40 yr old woman or was he making polite conversation? And anyways if he was interested what could they possible have in common? What would people think? Cradle robber, desperate old lady, the thoughts raced through her mind, but then again why not, men date younger women all the time and they get a high five so what was so different about her situation? As these thoughts ran through Claudia's mind reality hit her, she was probably over reacting to nothing and she started to feel foolish. Claudia made her way home that night straight to bed and as her head hit the pillow she fell fast asleep.

A couple of weeks had passed and curiosity was surely killing the cat! Claudia asked Lola if she was up for drinks that Friday night at Lulu's and of course she couldn't tell her dear friend no so it was a date. Lola found it a bit odd that Claudia asked Hank if he wanted to join them and to invite some friends along, that in it's self struck Lola odd because they couldn't stand Hank, but then again she was up for anything Claudia had in mind, it always seemed like a mini adventure.

Claudia rushed home to change, she had to look just right, just in case Craig showed up, didn't want to look desperate and out dated, but like always she pulled it off, besides she was a fashion designer she knew how to accessorize without going overboard. Lola decided that she would meet her at the bar instead of her apartment so Claudia left a little earlier than usual. Her heart was pounding with excitement and she started to feel ridiculous, childish, then out right stupid. Nothing was going to happen that night and even if he did show it wasn't for her. It was something she was going to have to see for herself, rejection wasn't something she liked to face but it was something she could handle. Besides the odds of him going were slim how could he show up not knowing that she was a tad bit interested? She was going to go anyways and relax and relieve some stress if he showed he showed, and if he didn't it wasn't meant to be but a wishful thought.

Claudia walked into Lulu's and strutting in right behind her was Lola. It was November so it was quite cold. Lola was a bit annoyed that Claudia had her coming out in this cold weather she knew that she was up to something because this was really out of the ordinary for Claudia, but as long as trouble didn't linger Lola was in. Claudia casually glanced around to see if Craig was anywhere, and of course he wasn't not even Hank. They ordered the usual's and sat at the bar by the pool tables 30 minutes passes when Hank walked in with Craig, Claudia's heart was beaten faster than she could count. She had to approach this situation in a calm matter, she didn't want to seem desperate. Craig walked up to Lola first and said hello then turned to Claudia, "When Hank asked me to come I was hoping that you would be here" Claudia melted, "I like older women" So how was Claudia gonna respond to that? The night went on casual they talked and laughed. Hank was very clingy to Claudia that night and it threw everybody off. Craig talked to Lola that night and Claudia found herself playing pool with Hank, that's not the way it was suppose to happen, did Craig get the wrong impression? Did he think that I was interested in Hank? Claudia sat there disappointed as the night was coming to an end. Out of curiosity and stupidity Claudia gave Hank her email and agreed to keep in touch, it was not something she anticipated but after a few cosmos and no response from Craig it seemed like a good idea.

Holiday's had passed and it was already the second week in February, work was going well and Claudia had been busier than ever. She was going threw her emails when she came across one from a unfamiliar address, it said hey stranger how are you? When she continued to read the small message she realized that it was from Craig. A bolt of excitement ran through her spine and it took her a while to take hold of herself. She responded back with a short message: Hey you, long time no see. They responded back to each other with small sentences like, how are you, what are you doing, what happened that night, good question what did happen that night? Claudia responded with "I thought you were interested in Lola the way you two talked? No Craig responded just friendly conversation. What about you and Hank? Hank? No, no, no Claudia responded, he's an arrogant idiot, not my type, Craig laughed on email with hahaha. There was a long email pause, you know the one that takes at least 20 minutes to respond back, you sit and stare at the computer, waiting, running to get a drink, waiting some more, then there it appears: "you still there?" Craig ask "of course" Claudia responds, "can I have your number" another pause . . . Claudia gives him the number and wonders if this is a mistake.

Two days passed and Craig finally calls Claudia on the phone, she couldn't believe that he actually called and he couldn't believe that she actually gave him the number. There was a sense of awkwardness first with Claudia, he was 16 years younger than her besides sex what could they possible have in common? Craig was very fascinated with Claudia, in his eyes what could this beautiful woman possibly find attractive in him? She never realized that all her fears were instilled in him as well. He was feeling bolts of energy flowing through his body as she talked to him. Neither one of them had no idea that what was about to happen was going to change there lives forever . . . .

Craig stood about 5'10" he was slender with a light complexion. He was hispanic with dark brown hair, his facial hair had a tint of blond that you can catch when the sun hit his face. He had two sleeves of tattoos that covered his arms from the shoulders down. He had the fullest perfect set of lips a man could have with the sexiest smile that would melt your heart away, He was a young guy born and raised in the Bronx, he had a brother who was serving a 5 yr sentence for robbery. Craig also moved into his mother's house to help pay with monthly expenses, he wasn't a troubled teen growing up but where he grew up it was inevitable that trouble was going to follow him. He was happy with his life but Craig felt something was missing. He had a on again off again relationship with a girl for six years and the love he thought he had was beginning to die down. He had a blue collar job that entailed hard labor, he worked in the shipping department at Macy's. It wasn't a high paying job but it payed his bills. Everyday after work Craig would head down to Gino's house, one of the boys that grew up in the neighborhood, and soon after, all the boys would show up to sit around drink and do the usual things. It was a everyday occasion that was getting very old to Craig, he needed to get out, get away, but how? It's something that just didn't happen in the Bronx, you were branded for life or so he thought.

On the night Craig met Claudia it was supposed to be a short night. Craig had intentions to walk in and talk to Hank about a job that he had heard about in Manhattan, but when Craig walked into Lulu's that night he had no idea that there was going to be a woman that was going to take his breath away. When he took one look at Claudia he was left speechless and for the reasons he walked into that bar that night, were long forgotten and being in her presence was all he wanted.

Craig always was attracted to women with meat on there bones, the skinny framed women never caught his attention. He liked women with long dark hair and Claudia's just shined so pretty that attracted him. Her curvacious body, thick legs, her butt that stuck out like two perfect bubbles, not saggy or spread out like butter on bread, just perfectly round and big enough to fit her body frame. To him she was the closes thing to perfection he had ever seen in a woman and he was destined to meet her. Craig was not a shy person, as a matter of fact he was quite the comedian himself, but when he found himself around Claudia he shut down. Her presence gave him a sense of unworthiness, not because she made him feel that way but because of how he felt towards her, how could someone so educated and talented be interested in him, Little did he know that deep down Claudia was feeling the same, the attraction they shared was electrifying and ready to be challenged.

February was coming to an end and Claudia was getting ready for a trip down to Dallas. There was this big fashion show and Claudia's haulters were going to be showcased on the runway. It was a exciting time for her and busy as well. She was going to be gone for a week so to pass the time she decided to take Lola. Lola was a funny character, always ready for excitement but in a low key kind of way. She liked the drama as long as she wasn't part of it. So to go on a trip with Claudia was something she could not pass up. The gossip, people with no fashion sense always made interesting conversation for her. It was going to be hetic but fun at the same time. It was a mini vacation that the both of them were anxious to share.

Claudia had been talking to Craig now for a week or two on the phone till 2 in the morning, so getting up in for work was getting to be more of a hassel. They stayed talking on the phone for hours, talking about work, fashion, there past times, the list went on and on. Craig was a little disappointed that Claudia was leaving, they haven't seen each other since the last time they met at Lulu's and he was longing to see her, she was anxious to see him too but traveling to Dallas was a opportunity she had to take so Craig would have to wait. Claudia and Lola arrived at 3:00 in the afternoon at Kenedy airport. It was raining and cool in Dallas, nothing like New York weather, it was doing a terrible number on there hair but with everything going on hair was the last thing on there minds. Claudia booked them a room at a 4 star hotel and Lola was estatic. See Claudia had high expections and expensive good taste, to a certain extent, so even though she wasn't rich she was able to maintain a comfortable way of living and when she had to go out of town she spared no expense on making there stay as comfortable as possible. Lola loved it! They checked in and decided to eat at a resturant in the downtown area of Dallas. Claudia was in the mood for steak and Lola wanted Mexican Food, scince they were in Texas Lola felt she had to take in all the Mexican Food she could because New York mexican cuisine did not add up to Texas mexican cuisine so with that in mind Claudia gave in to Lolas craving of mexican food and found a cute resturant called "Rosarios" it was nice, small, not your upscale fine dining but nice and clean so Claudia felt comforable eating there. As the girls sat there they ordered some margaritas and as they where waiting, a tall hispanic male walked up to there table and introduced himself to Lola. He was a good looking man about the same age, dark hair, green eyes, carmel color, not light, medium built, that smelled so manly that Lola was drooling all over the qucamole, (avacado)! He turned and introduced himself to Claudia, "Hi my name is Antonio Huerta, I recognized your photo on the program for Saturdays fashion show, I am the fashion director and I wanted to introduce myself personnally and tell you how interesting and different your vision of fashion is" Usually by this time Claudia would be drooling and speechless with such an atractive man coming up to her, but she didn't feel that, in fact she felt nothing, no excitement no nothing, all she could think about was Craig. She thanked him for the complement and proceeded to drink her margarita, with no invitation from her, he grabbed a chair and sat down at her table, Lola couldn't be happier, Claudia on the other hand felt annoyed by him, it really wasn't his fault but she just could not get into his conversation. As he dragged his words Claudia's mind drifted off remembering the first time she saw Craig, she excused herself to the bathroom and decided to call him besides it wouldn't be rude Lola seemed to be enjoying herself and Mr. Huerta was caught in her conversation so it was the perfect time.

As fast as she could get the phone out of her purse she started dialing Craig's number praying he would answer, he did. It was the most pleasant to hear, his voice. They talked for a while and she confessed that she missed talking to him, before she could finish her sentenced he also confessed that he missed her voice. Hearing that made her quiver, the more she talked to him the more she longed for him. In her mind all she really wanted to do was go back home so she could see him instead of talking to him on the phone, nonetheless this was something she had to do and the sooner she was able to get through this the sooner she was home.

Claudia headed back to the table, Lola stepped out for a while because she received a phone call from a guy Claudia had no idea she was talking to, so Claudia was left to entertain Mr. Huerta something she dreaded but did because he was director of the fashion show. Mr. Huerta offered to pay for dinner and of course Claudia refused but Mr. Huerta was being so presistant that to shut him up she gave in. There was a awkward silence between them that seemed like forever but as Claudia was getting ready to excuse herself Lola walked back in. Friday night, Claudia, Lola, and some of the other fashion guru's decided to hit the night life so without any concern on how Claudia felt, Lola invited Antonio. With a smile he responded with a very simple yes and said that he would have a limo waiting for them to pick them up and take them anywhere there hearts desired. Lola couldn't wait, Claudia on the other hand was not impressed but she didn't want to ruin the party so she smiled and said a simple thank you.

Friday was a hetic day full of sewing and sizing making sure that her halters were perfect to the fit. She had to hire plus size models and that she loved doing. It beat hiring those skinny no shape models that were completely clueless and full of themselves. Besides beauty comes in curves not bones. Claudia was exhausted but she did promise Lola a good time so with that in mind she headed back to the hotel to get ready for her night out with the girls, not to thrilled she had to get herself in the mood and be the life of the party that she usually was so with a warm shower it would do the trick. She wore a black blouse low cut not to revealing with diamond studs that she designed herself, with a pair of black slacks and black heeled boots, simple yet moderately sexy. Lola wore a black skirt that Claudia designed just for her with a white laced top that wrapped her just right, conservative yet sassy. As they headed out to the lobby the limo pulled up and Mr. Huerta opened the door. The girls entered the limo with the rest of the ladies of fashion and proceeded to hit one of Dallas hottest nightclubs, a little exciting but not impressive at least not to Claudia.

In the limo was champagne, and all the high priced alcohol you could think of, the girls went crazy. Usually Claudia would be in the mix laughing and mixing up a cosmo or two but not this time. She was missing Craig's voice. She wanted to see him and see what he was like in person. She talked to him several times on the phone and fell for him like that so she wondered by meeting with him what level would that take her? Nonetheless it wasn't going to happen that night so she came back to reality and poured herself a drink. As they drove into the clubs driveway the girls exit out the limo one by one, Claudia was the last person to exit the limo, Antonio stopped her. "Your mind seems to be else where, is there anything I can help you with?" "Not empurticular" Claudia responded so with that Antonio let her go and walked her into the nightclub. The night went on and the girls were having a great time with the exception of Claudia, she couldn't get Craig out of her mind! Antonio tried his hardest to get her attention. He asked her to dance, bought her a drink, tried to make conversation and nothing worked. The music annoyed her, all she wanted to do was talk to Craig. Before the night was over Antonio finally asked Claudia "Was there something I said to offend you?" "I've tried everything to get your attention and you simply shoot me down, all the time?" Claudia responded, "Look Mr. Huerta you seem like a very nice man but back home I'm talking to someone and I really don't seem myself interested in anyone else." "Ouch" he responded, "I can respect that, well who ever he is must be very special to have such a beautiful woman fall all over him, good luck to you and to him." And with that he walked away. Claudia sat there in amazement with herself, what was she thinking, it was just simple conversation on the phone, how could she let herself get caught up with someone she hasn't yet dated? This was worse than she thought, the hard shell she had over her heart was finally breaking off little by little. She could hardly understand what was happening to her but she was anxious to take the first step and find out. Claudia could her a group of girls laughing as they approached her, Lola with a smile from ear to ear. She was happy to see that Lola had a good time so with that they headed out the door.

13

Saturday finally came and the show was a success. There was small time celebrities there that Claudia and Lola met such as the wife of one of the banks there in the city, the mayors wife, and the governors, some playboy bunnies, and the Dallas Cowboy Cheerleaders. It was fun but both girls were glad it was over. Claudia decided to catch a early flight back she couldn't wait to hear Craigs voice. Lola slept on the plane back heading home, she was still a bit hung over from the night before.

Chapter 2

As the plane hit solid ground in the big apple, Claudia's heart began to beat fast, she couldn't wait to hear Craig's voice, it was the one thing that kept her going this trip. Claudia and Lola picked up there luggage and flagged down a taxi, Lola was the first person to be dropped off. With a big hug goodbye Lola thanked Claudia for everything and exited out of the car. "See you Monday Lola shouted" "Yup back to reality" Claudia responded.

The taxi finally arrived in front of Claudia's apartment she was so happy to be back home but even happier knowing that in a while she would hear Craig's voice. She paid the taxi driver and darted up the stairs, purse and luggage flapping everywhere. She stumbled trying to unlock the door but finally got it open. She threw her bags on the floor, kicked off her shoes, jumped on her bed and started to dial Craig's number. The phone rang a couple of times when she finally heard "Hello". "Hey" Claudia responded "how are you stranger" "She could hear the excitement in his voice, "I was beginning to wonder if you were ever coming back" he laughed and so did she. "So when do I finally get to see you?" Craig asked Claudia, "How about tonight, there's a real nice place that I heard about called Cabo's it's located right in the heart of Manhattan, I hear they serve great martini's" "I never had a martini" Craig responded "But I'm willing to try it out", "Sounds good, how does nine sound?" "Perfect" Craig answered, and they hung up. Claudia fell out of bed with excitement bumping her head on the floor she was so ecstatic that she didn't feel a bump swelling up on the side of her head. It was 7 in the evening and she had two hours to make herself presentable for him. She wanted to look sophisticated yet sexy, she could hardly wait.

Claudia arrived at Cabo's 10 minutes early and as she walked in Craig was already there waiting for her, dressed in fitted but not to fitted jeans, nicely pressed, a long sleeve colared blue and white stripped shirt with buckled shoes, he smelled so good, a manly scent that lingered just right around her nose "Hey" Claudia said "Hey" Craig responded "It feels good to finally have you for myself" he said. "Yes I know I've been so busy and with my line of tops going out it's been hectic" They sat down at a table in the middle of the bar, Claudia ordered a Cosmo and since Craig never had that before he decided to try one. It was a mixture of vodka, cranberry juice, triple sec, and a twist of lime, Claudia's favorite. Craig seemed to like it too. As the time went by both of them talked and laughed for hours and between all that, they couldn't help but to stare into each other's eyes. At that moment Claudia fell head over heals and she wondered if he was feeling the same.

Claudia talked about her job and her fashion line, she could go on for hours talking about that. Craig sat there and listen to her every word. Everything that came out of her mouth fascinated him. Everytime she stopped talking Craig wanted her to say more. It made her feel special that someone was actually interested in what she had to say. After a while Claudia stopped talking and said to Craig "Enough on me I want to hear more about you and your job, your life." Craig smiled but deep inside he didn't want to tell her to much. He felt that If he really told her what his life was really like she wouldn't want anything to do with him. A fashion designer with a guy with no excitement other than drinking at Gino's, he wasn't ready to let her know much about that. So with respect he responded with "There's not much to tell compared to you, I want to hear everything about you before I bore you". They laughed and with that Claudia continued her conversation.

It was going to be midnight, but in New York that's still early. It didn't matter that they had to get up early that evening, neither one of them was ready to leave each others company so they decided to go uptown to a upscale martini bar that Claudia was dieing to go to but never made the time to do, it was called the Pink Dreams Martini Lounge. As Craig and Claudia headed out of Cabo's to Pink Dreams as they turned the corner laughing and acting like teenagers, a sound of thunder filled the sky and the unexpected rain began to come down hard hitting them like tiny little spears falling from the sky. Neither one of them could care less that they were drenched. They made it to Pink Dreams and to there surprise no one was there but a bartender and the owner. "Welcome to Pink Dreams, my name is Scott the owner of this place, it's usually never this empty but I guess they got word of the rain so everyone decided to stay in for the night" they all laughed and Scott responded "first round is on the house what'll it be", two cosmos, Craig answered. "Good choice that's a sign of a sophisticated woman, have them ready for you in a bit". The atmosphere was very cozy. It was a candle lit place with rock walls and columns. There were leather sofas surrounding tables and the scent of cigars filled the room. It was a very sophisticated place and Claudia felt right at home. Craig and Claudia sat on a couch and Scott brought them there drinks. "What kind of music do you play here?" Craig asked. "On fridays it's Old school R&B and today's R&B," Claudia smiled because she loves that kink of music "and on saturdays' it's old skool hip hop and today's hip hop, you two look like you would fit right in, I suggest that you come by on a Saturday that's when it's really tight". "Sounds good" Craig responded "We will definitely be back". One thing that Claudia loved to do was to dance, it didn't matter to what but Pink Dreams was a place she definitely wanted to be part of.

They sat there awhile talking and laughing, the rain was still going strong, after a while it got a little quite. "I don't mean to sound pushy, but can I kiss you?" It was something Claudia was waiting to hear all night, "Yes, you may" she responded. Craig leaned over slowly caressing her arm and her hair like she was a fragile piece of art work, his lips slowly touching hers just as she had imagined. It wasn't a tongue kiss but a kiss of passion, a candy kiss, then slowly she felt herself let go. Her tongue slowly started to wrap around his, small candy kisses surrounding his lips, the intense so strong that neither one of them wanted to stop. After a long while of kisses they finally stopped, both staring deep into each others eyes amazed at what they both shared. "As much as I regret saying this I think it's time we go" Claudia said. "We both have work early in the morning and I don't want you falling asleep on the job" Craig, with a big grin on his face, agreed. They stood at the door at Pink Dreams staring at the rain that was still falling hard, "it's just rain, it's not like your gonna melt" Scott said, "I guess" Claudia replied. "Are you up to running in the rain?" Craig asked "We did it once we can do it again" Claudia responded. So off they ran through the rain once again hitting them like spears from the sky. Both of them laughing so hard that in the middle of the block they stopped to catch there breath. The excitement of the rain falling and the sense of being like teenagers again had them kissing so passionately in the rain. Craig pushed Claudia up against the brick wall and pressed his lips hard against hers, she felt his tongue run all around her lips while her body pulsed with a sense of fire and desire, the rain falling down like candy and there lips locked together sharing there candy kisses.

As the rain slowed down, so did the intensity of their kiss, Craig's forehead leaned into Claudia's forehead so he slowly backed away from her, both of them drained from all the desire they had for each other. As they stared at one another for awhile a big smiled consumed them both so they headed back to Cabo's walking in what felt like candy rain hitting there back instead of spears from the sky.

It was Monday morning, February the 28th the start to a wonderful morning. Even though Claudia was tired she felt rejuvenated and ready to start her day. She had new ideas for her spring line up and everyone around her seemed to have a positive karma, everything was perfect. Lola came walking down with her usual cup of coffee, "Where have you been, Miss Pris, you seem to be glowing this morning?" "I tried calling you last night and you were no where to be found, what is going on with you?" "Remember the night you and me went out to Lulu's and that tall slender guy walked up to

Hank, well I've been talking to him for a while and we finally went out yesterday!" Lola didn't look the bit surprise, "I'm all in everyone's business in the bar do you honestly think I'm not going to be in my friends biz, I was just waiting for you to tell, so tell" Claudia went on and on about him his smile, his lips, his tattoos that drove her crazy, and the night they shared, it was all magical. Lola had a client coming so she had to cut the conversation short, "Call me later girl so you can tell me more about Craig" "I will" Claudia replied.

As the day went by Claudia sent texts to Craig and he responded, they were like a couple of teenagers. Claudia was caught laughing by herself in a corner and on the other side of the text so was Craig, they were both caught up in there own little world. It was seven in the evening and Claudia was finishing up the last of her paperwork. Craig on the other hand ended his day at 6 so he was hoping that Claudia would meet him for a bite to eat or something. As Claudia was saying goodbye to the doorman her phone rang, it was Craig. "Hey" Claudia answered, "Hey" Craig replied for some reason he loved when she answered the phone that way and he mimicked her to poke fun. Being that Claudia was extemely tired she asked for a rain check on dinner and Craig understood, he himself was feeling tired more than usual. They hung up with sweet goodbyes and Claudia fell fast asleep with Craig on her mind hoping he was doing the same.

March fastly approached and was ending fast. Craig and Claudia talked everyday, they always had something to say and everything that Claudia said fascinated Craig. She was funny even when she wasn't trying to be. Craig found himself spending more time with Claudia than with his boys. They couldn't understand what he saw in a 40 year old woman, "She's gonna shrivel before you hit your prime" they would tease, "not my girl" he would respond. Since they were his boys they really didn't have much to say, they saw a difference in Craig and left him alone, for now.

Claudia had a weekend show coming up in the Bronx on the 26th of March, it also marked one month that Craig and Claudia had been talking and since Craig was from the Bronx he thought it would be nice to have a room for her in one of those fancy 4 star hotels she loved so much, it was going to break him but he wanted to do something special for her the way she deserved to be treated. He just wasn't sure if Claudia would take it the wrong way, she was different than all the girls he dated and he didn't want to treat her like them.

Craig talked to Claudia that night and told her that he really wanted to reserve a room for her so she wouldn't have to take the subway home late at night after the shows. Claudia's heart filled with excitement, "Are you planning to stay with me those days I'm there?" Craig's heart filled with excitement also "I hadn't thought of it, but it would be nice to spend time with you." "Great then it's settled you can stay with me while I'm there and after my shows you can show me where you grew up in the Bronx, I've never been around long enough to embrace it." Craig had butterflies in his stomach nobody was ever interested in his life especially where he came from, he was happy.

The weekend was finally here and Claudia was more excited than ever. It wasn't for the fact that her clothing line had exploded it was the fact that she was going to spend the weekend with Craig. Here heart filled with joy and desire just thinking about it. Now while all this was going on with Claudia Lola was involved with a guy of her own. Just like several trips before Lola was going to attend this one as well, the only difference is she was taking a guest.

Claudia shipped all her clothing line the night before, so all she had to do was board the subway to the Bronx, it was 5:00 in the evening when Claudia and Lola arrived, Craig was there to greet them. Craig stood there in his blue denim jeans and blue collared work shirt, he looked tired and sexy, Claudia was always turned on by a hard working man, and that's exactly what she saw when she looked at him. Craig gave Lola a quick hug then turned to hug Claudia, he held her tight for what seemed like a eternity. Claudia took a deep breath to smell the sweet scent of his body, his sweat had a mild musky odor that took her breath away. She was grateful that he didn't smell like a old moldy wet shirt that sat in a laundry basket for days, she was taken by his presence.

As they walked up the stairs to the street level Craig flagged down a taxi, the hotel was just four blocks away but Craig knew that the girls were tired from the train ride from Manhattan. Craig sat behind the driver, Claudia in the middle and Lola behind the passenger side, as they drove to the hotel Claudia tried to get a better look of the neighborhood and a feel of how Craig might of grown up. There were kids playing baseball in the street just like the movies, and on the street corner there was a flower stand with exotic flowers. Across the street there was a group of older women sitting on the steps laughing, sipping out of Styrofoam cups. Claudia didn't know if this is were Craig grew up but if it was it didn't look bad, the buildings did look old but in good shape and there didn't seem to be any bums on the corners like she expected. Not to bad she thought so why was he so hesitant to talk about his upbringing? It was something she wasn't going to push, when he was ready, he would tell her.

As the taxi turned the corner Claudia was surprised to see a huge beautiful white building with large columns in the front, it had a huge waterfall in the middle of the entrance, Claudia had no idea that it was the hotel that Craig had reserved for them. Lola sat back laughing, "You knew about this didn't you?" Claudia asked Lola, "Of course, I needed to know how else was I going to book a room for me and Gabriel?" "Oh Gabriel, he has a name" Claudia responded sarcastically. As the three of them excited the car a small built guy in his late 30's stood there wearing a pair of jeans, t-shirt, and a baseball cap. He wasn't ugly just a plain everyday Joe you would bump into on the Texas streets, it was Gabriel. Lola introduced Craig and Claudia they all shook hands and preceded to the front desk. "Hi Mr. Perez, it's nice to see you back, I see you finally brought your lady," Claudia blushed and smiled. She never realized that his last name was Perez, he only had it tattooed from the top of his shoulder all the way down the side of his arm, Craig Perez it had a nice ring to it she thought.

The four of them went there separate ways and decided to met up for drinks later, they all were tired and wanted to rest before they ventured out into the night. Craig and Claudia's room was on the 10th floor as they entered the elevator to go to their room there was a strange silence between them that had not happened to them since they met, "Is everything OK" Claudia asked Craig, "Yes, I'm just a little tired, and overwhelmed, I can't believe you are here with me." As they entered the room both of them stood there a little surprised, the room was beautiful but there was two beds, Claudia wondered if maybe Craig was on a different level than her and Craig was red with embarrassment. "What a idiot, she probably thinks I did this on purpose." Claudia broke the ice by saying "We'll one's for sleeping and the other we can play cards" they both laughed and Craig felt more at ease. "My girl the comedian he thought."

Both of them started to unpack there luggage, Craig noticed that Claudia had 5 changes of clothes, shoes to go with every outfit, jewelry, perfume, and a huge makeup bag. All he brought was 1 pair of pants, two shirts that he had picked up from the cleaners, and two pair of boxers that he was embarrassed to even take out of the bag. Both of them finished unpacking and sat down on separate beds. Claudia started the conversation, "I don't mean to be a bother, but is everything OK? You seem so distant, not your usual self" Craig quiet at first responded, "I look at you and your beautiful, since I've met you I've never seen you wear the same thing twice, your skin is so soft, you smell good always. I watched you as you unpacked and your perfect. I look at myself and I have nothing but a faded pair of jeans, boxers that I wouldn't dare pull out, I look at myself and wonder what could you possible see in me?" Claudia waited before she responded she had to think very carefully how she was going to respond to this, "Craig when you see me, do you see a materialistic person, do you think that all I care about is money, clothes, expensive things? I have clothes because I'm a designer. I look at you and see a hard working ambitious man with a very big heart. When I first met you I fell for you because you were real, I don't see a egotistical male who worries about what other people think of him, I like you because you are who you are. You may not think much of yourself but to me you are a diamond in the rough." Wow, Craig sat there in amazement, he began to make his way over to the other bed and lean over to give her a soft kiss, she gave in and kissed him back slowly he started to lean his body into hers the kiss became more intense as he started to caress her face, he worked his way touching her hair and running his hand down her arm, her body was trembling with desire for him. He slowly moved his hand down into her pants rubbing and touching her ever so softly making her wet making her moan with intense desire for him. He slowly unbuckled her pants and slowly removed them from her as she lay there lost in her desire for him he unbuckled his pants and pulled out this beautiful piece of manhood, as he slowly entered her she could feel this pain of pleasure so deep, one that she had never experienced. What he had to offer was more than she could handle and a tear ran down her face, it was a extreme sense of pain that jolted her whole body, as he kissed her he swayed into her slowly back and forth then as he went faster she could feel herself swell ready to explode. She squeezed her pelvis tight and wrapped her vagina tight around him, he felt this sensation run down his spine his body began to quiver and he started to moan with a deep desire for her. Together they released themselves with a intensity so deep that neither one of them could stop.

Craig slowly lay-ed his head on Claudia's chest, both overwhelmed, Craig turned over to lay on his back. As the both of them lay-ed there staring into the ceiling, Claudia's cell phone rang, it was Lola. "So what time are you guys coming down for dinner?" By this time both Craig and Claudia were exhausted but neither one of them wanted to be rude, besides they really hadn't met Gabriel and thought it wouldn't be fair to do that to Lola, so they decided to get up and get dressed both with a huge smile on there face. As they made there way down to dinner, Lola could see a glow in Claudia's face, without saying a word, she smirked at her friend as Claudia smirked back Lola knew without words, exactly what had happened and she couldn't be more happy for her friend.

Chapter 3

It was 6 in the morning Saturday and Claudia woke up with Craig starring right at her, with a small laugh he tells her, "Good morning gorgeous," "Good morning" Claudia responded. "I have to go to work for a couple of hours this morning but I promise I will make it back in time for us to spend some time together before your big fashion show tonight. So what I want you to do is go back to sleep and wait for me, I'll be back before you know it." With a offer like that it wasn't hard for Claudia to agree. This was probably the first time she even stayed in to sleep so she was happy he suggested it. Claudia got out of bed to walk him to the door, Craig still had a hard time grasping the thought that she was actually here with him, and Claudia was having a hard time believing that anybody could be that wonderful. As she kissed him goodbye, she locked the door and walked back to the bed to go to sleep, as she closed her eyes all she could do was think of the night before, it gave her goosebumps as she slowly fell back asleep.

It was almost noon when Claudia heard a knock at the door, she woke up startled and realized it was probably Craig. He stood there smiling with a bag in his hand, "hungry?" "Of course" she replied "I can't believe that I stayed asleep this long!" Craig responded "Well why not? I mean you definitely don't need any beauty rest but you sure do work a lot, and your body was probably craving it." "I guess your right, I never realized how tired I was." and with that said Claudia began to take the food out the bag. If there was one thing Craig like to do, it was to eat. As thin as he was you wondered where he packed on all that food. He also liked a woman that wasn't embarrassed to eat herself. One time Craig took a girl out to dinner and when it was time to order, she ordered a side salad, rabbit food what he likes to call it, and a glass of water with a splash of lemon. Craig got so turned off by that, that he himself lost his appetite, he excused himself and said he had a emergency and walked out. As Claudia took out two greasy burgers from the bag he was happy to see that she was far from being embarrassed to eat with him, he loved it!

Craig and Claudia were sitting on two different beds laughing and making fun of the commercials that were coming out on the T.V., Claudia noticed that Crag's cell phone kept ringing like crazy, he would glance at it and ignore it, Claudia didn't think to much about it but it was starting to annoy her. After awhile Craig started to get a little serious, he stared at Claudia for a long time, he asked her "Do you ever wonder more about me, I know I haven't told you much and I admit I've been hesitant to tell you but after being around you as much as I have I feel like I need to tell you how life is for me."

Claudia answered him, "Yes I wonder why it's so hard for you to talk about yourself and your family, and I want to know that part about you but I figured when your ready you will tell me." With that said Craig without hesitation began to tell her is life story.

Craig began telling her that he grew up in a tough side of town in the Bronx, it was his mother, his little brother and himself, Craig was the oldest. His mother always found ways to make ends meet but it was hard for her raising two boys on her own. Craig's dad was in prison for possession of firearms and he wasn't looking to get paroled at least for another 10 more years. As a youngster Craig liked to attend school but as he got older things started to change. He started to hang around with the wrong crowd and little mischievous things turned into big mischievous things. He never got in to trouble with the law but only because he never got caught, there was plenty of chases for him and his boys and the more they got away, the more they wanted to push it.

When Craig got to High School he started getting a little tired of all the negative in his life, he wanted to take a more serious route, but by this time, no adult took him serious except for one administrator that he will never forget, Mr. Forbes. Mr. Forbes would call Craig into his office every chance he got talking to him, encouraging him. One day he asked Craig what he would like to do and Craig said "play football" So that's what Mr. Forbes did, helped him get into football. So for his four years of high school he played. Craig continued to go down the right path and it paid off, he graduated from high school and that was a big accomplishment for him considering the path he was taking, but when he graduated trouble seemed to linger and wait for him.

Craigs younger brother was on the same path as he was but he continued down the wrong path and because of that Craig felt like he needed to stick around the boys in the neighborhood so he could keep a eye on his little brother. One day his little brother decided to rob a convenience store at gunpoint, nobody got hurt but a chase accured and eventually he got caught, it cost him 6 years of his life, so since then Craig felt stuck in the circle.

Craig continued to talk and Claudia continued to listen, "Have I scared you away yet?" he asked, "No, why would you say that?" she answered "I'm not going anywhere just yet." She laughed. He paused and with a deep breath he continued his story he continued to tell her that about three years ago he was outside on his steps when 3 guys, who he knew from down the street not really on a personal note, walked by and started harrassing him, he ignored them and decided to go inside, later on that evening he was meeting with a lady friend and as he was walking down his front steps those three guys drove by and shot him with a 12 gauge shot gun, hitting him in the stomach shattering his spleen and putting a big hole in him, he was on a respirator for 2 days, he almost died, his mom never leaving his side. He thought he would never walk again. Luckily he did survive but it left him with a big scare from his belly button all the way down. Claudia was left speechless, she was with him the night before but didn't even notice his scar.

There was a awkward silence in the room, then Craig spoke, "Do you see now why I didn't want to share my life with you? How can someone so educated and beautiful, so perfect want anything to do with a guy like me?" "A guy like you?" Claudia said "A guy who is so wonderful to me, a guy who makes me feel like a million bucks, a guy as sexy as you? Why wouldn't I want it any other way?" "Then there is one more thing that I think I should tell you" Claudia's heart fell.

Craig started to tell her that for 6 years he was involved with a girl that he loved very much and just recently they broke up. He assured her that it was over and all he wanted to do was move on. He went on to describe there relationship, she was also from the neighborhood, they met in school and had a off again on again relationship. He continued to tell her that she was a tough girl herself, she was attracted to his life style and together they went through it. One thing that Craig noticed about Claudia is she did not like to argue, if he told her he was heading to Gino's house to have a beer or two, she'd hang up with a simple "OK just be careful." Roxanne, the name of his ex would have a fit, curse him out with a mouth like a trucker, and continue to tell him how worthless he was. Within the past two years all they did was argue it seemed the only reason she would come around was to get high and hang around the boys. She had no ambition and no sense, Craig was getting very tired of that. He longed to sit and converse with someone who sounded like they knew what they were talking about. Craig took a deep breath and stopped talking. After a long hesitation Claudia began to speak.

"It sounds like you've had a tough childhood but you seem to have made it out OK, your doing good for yourself. Everybody has problems within there families nobody's perfect and believe me my family is far from being perfect themselves, you shouldn't be ashamed of who you are or where you've come from. As far as your Ex it's gonna take time but if your serious about letting her go it's gonna get easier as time goes by, you just need to be patient." Craig sat there in amazement, Claudia was the most wonderful person he had ever met, any other girl would have been out the door after hearing his story especially about his ex, what more could he ask for. Craig interrupts her, "Honey where have you been all my life, you always seem to amaze me" Claudia responded "well had I been in your life any sooner they probably would of arrested me for having a relationship with a minor! So to me I think the timings perfect." Both of them started to laugh, "Well lucky for me" Craig said.

Seven o'clock rolled around really fast and before you knew it Claudia and Craig found themselves rushing out the door to make it to the fashion show on time. Making there way downstairs, Lola and Gabriel where waiting for them. A taxi was already there so they jumped right in and headed down to the show. Craig had never seen so many people, so many sophisticated people waiting to see a line of clothing. He himself liked to dress up from time to time, he owned a few labeled garments but nothing like Claudia. He was really intrigued and fascinated with this side of her, she talked about her shows but to be part of it threw him back in amazement. As they sat down, in the front row of course, the show began, he was waiting to see a bunch of skinny women parading around in clothes trying to look sexy, remember Craig in not fascinated by skinny women it's the girls with meat on there bones that he likes. To his amazement when the big lights went out and the music started, there they come, plus size women! Plus size beautiful women, his baby was a genius! Putting a show together with her clothing line making those women look immaculate made him fall even more. His respect for her grew even deeper. As the show came to an end, Claudia was exhausted but happy with the outcome. There was a after party at the hotel were they were staying so they decided to go. Gabriel and Lola, Craig and Claudia had the time of there lives. It was an open bar so Craig and

Claudia were hitting up those Cosmos like they were water and the music was so alive, you hardly saw them sitting down, they danced the night away. Lola and Gabriel decided that they were gonna call it a night, Craig and Claudia decided to stay around a little longer. That's one of the things that was great between the two of them they didn't need anybody else to have a good time, as long as they were together nobody else seemed to matter. It was the last call on alcohol that night and Craig and Claudia seemed to be a bit drunk, as they proceeded to make there way up the stairs Claudia stumbled over. With both of them laughing hysterically Craig pulled out his hand to help her up. They both made it to the room safely and as they kicked off there shoes they both tumbled on to the bed. Sharing a drunk kiss, (you know the ones that are all wet and tongue flinging around everywhere) and frantic pulling clothes off throwing them all over the room, both of them lay-ed there butt naked and before you know it they both passed out.

As the sun came up that Sunday morning both of them were feeling sick to there stomach obviously hung over from the night before. Claudia opening her eyes slowly, realized that she had no clothes on. Trying to recall if anything had happened she was almost sure that it didn't and she could breath knowing that she didn't make a complete fool of herself. Craig began to open his eyes and realized the same, he was naked and a rush of heat began to fill his face with embarrassed. Claudia, to break the awkwardness asked "So did you have a good time last night?" "More than you'll ever know" Craig replied. "Well then great, lets get up shower and head down for breakfast, I'm sure Lola's waiting for us wanting to know all the dirty details." Craig answered with "Well Love let's do this, we work better as a team!" With that said Claudia started her morning.

As they checked out of the hotel Craig gave Claudia a big hug. "I don't want you to go, are you sure your gonna be OK? I don't mind riding with you on the subway back to Manhattan." Claudia answered him back "No I'll be OK, I'm not by myself remember Lola is riding back with me, besides you need to get some rest for work tomorrow, we've had a long weekend and you need to rest." With all that said they said there good byes and Claudia promised that she would call him when she got home . . .

Both very tired once again, Lola thanked Claudia for a great weekend, "I don't know if I'll see you at work tomorrow" Claudia told Lola, "What" Lola replied, "You never call in for work, are you feeling OK?" "Yes" Claudia replied "I'm just tired and I don't feel like going to work, I think the success of my show allows me one free pass off, don't you think?" "Don't look at me" Lola replied "I'm glad your coming to your senses for once, enjoy your day girl, you do deserve it" "Bye, talk to you later" Claudia responded.

Chapter 4

As Claudia promised she called Craig that night to let him know that she was home safe. They talked for a few minutes then hung up with sweet goodnights, they were both exhausted. The next morning Claudia woke up with a loud knock at the door, it was 6 in the morning and she couldn't even begin to guess who it could be. To her surprise it was Craig standing there in his work uniform soaking wet holding a bag from McDonalds, "hungry?" for him Claudia thought, and trying to sound as sexy as she responded, "of course I am." As he stood at the doorway Claudia asked him, "is it raining?" "No baby I just like coming over straight out of the shower smelling super clean for you" Claudia responded with a little chuckle, "sometimes I wonder about you, come on in and get dried up, so we can eat"

Craig walked in with so much confidence that it made Claudia melt, the way he carried himself made her feel good inside for some reason. In her eyes she saw a humble guy, what you see is what you get, no surprises and she was happy that she found somebody that way. Craig continued a conversation taking the food out of the bag when he noticed Claudia frowning, "What's a matter love you don't like fast food?" Claudia responded "Well to be honest with you, No, I like fine dining and I rather cook than eat fast food, it gives me heartburn." Craig felt a little stupid after saying all that, of course his girl didn't like fast food, she orders cosmos for christ sakes and likes 5 star hotels, what made him think she liked fast food?

Claudia could see the rush of red in his face, so to ease the embarressment Claudia comforts Craig by putting his face between her hands, "Hey why not eat fast food?" Claudia responds with excitement in her voice, "Let's enjoy the breakfast together, that's the main idea right?" "Well yes" Craig responded "Are you sure, I don't want you getting sick" "No of course not, Ill be fine." So with that Craig and Claudia sat down to eat there breakfast, both of them laughing and enjoying there early morning together, fogetting the embarrassement of earlier.

As they finished up breakfast Claudia could hear the rain on the window pane so she proceeded to tell Craig that she was contemplating going to work or not when the phone rang, It was the office reminding her of her 10 oclock appointment with the marketing director of Walmart. "There goes my plans for a free day" Claudia says "theres other days love" Craig responded. Did she hear correctly? A couple of times this morning he refered to her as love. Her heart began to swell with joy as she walked him to the door "how about dinner tonight?" Claudia asked Craig "Sure, anywhere emperticular?" Craig asked "As a matter of fact yes, Do you like Italian?" "I'll eat anything" Craig responded "Then great it's a date and it's on me" Claudia said with a smile. "NO! I can't let you pay." Craig insisted. "Don't worry it's ok I don't mind, besides it's fancy and scince I picked it I'll pay." "So what are trying to say, I can't handle fancy?" Craig said firmly "No that's not what Im saying, ok look fine you pay, ok? And all I want to do is show you a different side of what's out there besides your private element, no harm?" Craig didn't feel insulted he knew that eventually this was going to happen, it was one of the things that he liked so much about Claudia, her high maintenance appearance and expensive taste so he was excited to see how the other side keeped entertained.

Claudia's meeting went very well that morning and Craig had a busy day himself. Craig clocked out at 6 when he called Claudia. "You still at work love?" "As a matter of fact, I'm heading home right now as we speak" Claudia responded. "Give me a hour to get ready" Craig responded "Ummmm love I think I need a little more time, can I pick you up at 8?" Claudia found that a bit odd but agreed "8 is fine baby" "Ok see you then my love" Craig responded. See Craig didn't want to tell Claudia that he liked to take his time when he was getting ready to go out on a date or even with the boys. At the hotel room Craig had to put himself on speed control because they were on a time frame, but a normal night for him consist of a hour shower, he shaves his face, has to tuck in his shirt perfectly, cannot be any bubble coming out the back, has to brush his teeth, put cologne a certain way, and yeah cant forget the most important thing his hair, he has a ritual that he does everytime he brushes his hair. WOW, see nobody is perfect. So after all that grooming Craig was ready to pick up Claudia.

Craig showed up right on time and Claudia was ready to go. Craig wore black loose fitted jeans, a dark blue shinny collared long sleeved shirt with some black shoes. You could smell the Armani on him not to strong but not to faint either, he smelled so good that Claudia wanted to melt just smelling him. Claudia wore black straight fitted pants with red black stilettos, she had a long sleeved red silk blouse that wrapped around her body and criss crossed across her breast, her breast just popping out just enough to leave to the imagination.

Craig starred at her with amazement and admiration "you are so sexy" Craig responds, "Stop it, you must not get out much" Claudia replied. "Trust me I get out enough to know that my girl is sexy, beautiful, smart, and ummmm" "OK, OK, so I'm sexy" Claudia responds with a overwhelming rush of red on her face. "well if you haven't noticed your not to bad yourself" Claudia responds. "are you serious, I think I'm ugly" Craig says, "Not to me, I'm still trying to figure out what you see in this old lady." "Ha, ha funny can we go eat now?" And with that said Craig and Claudia headed out the door.

Craig flagged down a taxi and headed to Manicottis a very nice 5 star Italian restaurant. Craig was excited, he had never been to a place like that before, so he wanted to get a taste of the good life. The taxi stopped and Craig got off the taxi and walked around to open the door for Claudia. His mother always told him that was the thing to do with a woman of class, never thought he'd use it though, so he did just that. They walked up the stairs and the waiter greeted them, "table for two?" he asked "as a matter of fact we have reservations" Claudia responded. She gave them her name and he escorted them to a beautiful set table by the window that had a beautiful view of the city lights. The table was candlelit and Craig tried to hold his excitement, he was so nervous he wouldn't know how to act, that he was sweating immensely.

They both sat down and the waiter took there drink order. "I'll have some of your sweetest red wine" Claudia responded "and for you sir" the waiter asked Craig, "I'll have the same" He didn't' want to show that he had no idea what to order so he just went along with Claudia. After a few minutes of deciding what they wanted to eat the waiter took there order, Claudia order the spaghetti and meatballs and Craig ordered there specialty, Manicotti, as the waiter walked away Craig couldn't help but to stare at Claudia. "What?" Claudia says with a smirk, "I can't admire you?" Craig responds, "I'm just not use to it that's all, but go ahead and admire me all you want." Claudia laughed. Craig continued to stare at Claudia, after awhile he spoke in a very calm manner with the most serious look on his face that Claudia had never seen on him. "I hope I don't scare you away, but I have to tell you something, Everyday that I've been with you it's been great, we don't fight, you don't judge me, and you've open my eyes to other things in life that I really didn't care to explore until I met you. My heart melts when I see you and it aches when I'm not with you, I love you Claudia and I don't know how to deal with that in the sense that I want to keep you forever." Claudia's heart began to swell and tears filled her eyes. After a few seconds of silence she responded, "Craig when I first met you, you took my breath away. The only thing that might have stopped me from seeing you was the age difference but after I got to know you the age thing didn't matter to me, I was comfortable with us. You never made me feel older. We have so much in common and we don't need anyone to entertain us but us. Baby I've fallen in love with you too." After they both sat there and proclaimed there love to each other Craig moved everything on the table aside leaned over closely and whispered to her, "Can I kiss you" without a single word Claudia gave into his kiss and melted all over the manicotti . . .

After an hour talking and eating Claudia began to yawn. "Am I that boring?" Craig asked. "No, silly I'm just tired, it's been a long day, you can never bore me" "Well that's good to hear" Craig responds.

Claudia continues to tell Craig "Tomorrow I have a very short day I was wondering if maybe, if you'd like, I could take a trip down to the Bronx and hang out with you for a while" Craig was quiet for awhile when he finally responded, "Why are you so good to me? I've never met a girl who wasn't all about her, I'm so lucky, and yes I'd love for you to come over" "well great then I'll be over about 5 is that OK?" "anything for you" Craig responds.

The two of them finally finished dinner and called for there check, Craig was a little nervous to see what fine dinning cost him, after awhile the waiter came with the bill, slowly he opened the black book, $85.00! This was surely going to break him but he didn't care, his girl was worth every penny that he spent. "Is there anything else you would like?" the waiter asked Craig, "No that will be it, thank you sir." And with that Craig and Claudia rode a taxi back to Claudia's apartment.

It was a long night so Claudia kissed Craig goodnight, besides she was going to spend the evening with him tomorrow. Craig was a little disappointed but understood that Claudia woke up early in the mornings so he didn't want to cause any pressure so he kissed her back and starred back as the taxi drove away.

The next morning Claudia woke up more tired than usual, it was very hard for her to get out of bed, but she did and after a long hot shower she woke up and continued her morning ritual. She made it to work on time but seemed like forever making it there. On here desk was a pile of mail, and a stick it note from Lola. It read: Hey long lost friend, you think we can do lunch or does baby boy have priority? Ha, ha Claudia thought, I guess I can do lunch with this girl before she stalks me at home, Claudia laughed.

Claudia was getting ready for her spring line so she had a busy morning. She had planned to leave work at 12:00 so she decided to meet with Lola at 11:30 for lunch. They went to eat at a deli around the corner from the office. It was a light lunch, sandwich, chips, and a iced tea. It was enough to hold her till she meet up with Craig in the Bronx. The girls meet for an hour and caught up on things. Lola was having a bit of a financial problem so Claudia lend her a few dollars to help her get by, it was something that both of them did for each other. Lola was Claudia's only girlfriend so she felt she had to take care of her, they were like sisters.

Claudia finally departed from Lola and promised that she would call her when she arrived at the Bronx, she was so excited to see Craig that her stomach started to get upset. It was a long ride from Manhattan to the Bronx so she took some Tums to ease the ride. She arrived earlier than she had anticipated so she had to call Craig to meet her at the station. He felt so bad for not being there to greet her but it wasn't his fault Claudia had given him a later time. Craiged rushed to pick her up, she wasn't waiting that long but it seemed like a eternity to Claudia, she was anxious to see him.

As soon as Craig saw Claudia he ran up to her from behind and gave her a big hug. As he wrapped his arms around her she could smell his soft musky scent that drove her crazy. And Craig himself loved the way that she smelled. He always told her that he loved her scent and he hoped she never changed it. "So are you ready to go?" Craig asked Claudia, "Of course I am, I'm excited to see where you grew up!"

Chapter 5

Since Craig only lived 6 blocks away from the subway they decided to walk, Claudia wanted to get the feel of the city streets. It wasn't as busy as Manhattan and the people seemed friendlier, it didn't seem like a bad neighborhood just a older one that just needed a little tender love and care from the community, well at least that's what Claudia felt.

On the walk to Craig's house Claudia could feel that something was wrong but she really couldn't pin point the problem. "Are you OK Baby, you seem a little distant today" "really?" Craig responded, "No I'm OK, just tired I guess." Claudia stayed quiet and continued to walk. As they came closer to his house Craig responds, "Well there it is, home sweet home." It was brown brick, like the rest of the houses on the block, but it was clean and had a pretty wreath on the door, welcoming spring, the door itself was red, a pretty red, one window to the left of the door, "It's nothing fancy but it's home" Craig replied.

As Claudia walked in behind Craig she felt a sense of warmth through her body. It was a comfortable home. As you walked in to the right was the dining room with a nice table with 6 chairs, microwave cart and a picture of the last supper hanging over the microwave. To the side was a small kitchen but very well maintained, clean, with a scented candle burning on the counter top. To the right of that was the family room, it had a cute living room set with a small TV with no cable. The back room looked like a work room that had a dryer and the door to the back. To the left of the front door was the living room, it had a tan leather sofa and no TV, there was a long hallway and to the right was a bathroom and across from that was a bedroom and 3 others that followed as you walked the hall, Craig's room was the last one to the right. It was a nice room, he had a high queen size bed with a matching dresser and lamp table, everything seemed to be neat and clean. He didn't have anything on the walls but a picture of him and his boys, it was cozy.

"Would you like something to drink?" Craig asked Claudia, "Sure, what do you have?" "Not cosmos," Craig responds, "OK?" "Did I say something wrong, you seem a bit agitated to day?!" Claudia snaps. "Let's sit in the dining room I have something to tell you and I'm not sure if your gonna like me after I explain to you what I have to say." With that said Claudia's heart began to beat fast not knowing if this could possibly be the last night she would be seeing him.

Craig proceeded to talk, "Do you remember a while back I told you about my ex, Roxanne? Well after getting to know you

I realized that I cannot lie to you, so I feel I need to tell you that these couple of days have been real hard for me. Roxanne has a new boyfriend and I'm angry, after I met you I knew you were the one for me, but I have been with this girl a longtime, 6 years, and even though for the last 3 years it's been miserable, she's always had this power over me. I saw her the other day with her new boyfriend and it killed me! But then I saw your face and the old me would of gone after them both and I would of beat the living crap out of him, but then I remembered that I have you, and losing you meant more to me than getting her back, but it made me feel guilty for feeling that way towards her . . . . it confused me. I don't want to lose you but you are way out of my league and I wouldn't blame you if you decided to leave me."

Claudia didn't respond for a long time, she sat there took a sip of her ice water, looking straight into his eyes and began to talk, "I understand how you feel, it's hard to let go something or someone that you've loved for so long. There's something that I haven't told you because it hurts me so much to talk about it, but when I was 16 years old I fell in love with a boy who I loved dearly and married him when I was 17 against my parents wishes. We struggled together for many years but our love kept us going. When he was 25 he worked as a pumper on the oil fields going to the farmlands close to the border. On a hot night in August of 95, he was working the night shift when a big shoot out between the drug lords and the Mexican police took place, he didn't even know what hit him. A bullet shot him straight in the head and killed him instantly, it took officials 6 days to find him, the vultures found him first. My husband lay-ed there alone and that haunted me for a very long, long, long time. I never dated much after that and buried myself in my work, so I understand how hard it is to let go, but if it's not meant to be and she's just a bad habit that you have to break, she will always have that piece of your heart and you will never be happy."

Craig sat there speechless, "You never seem to amaze me, here I just poured out my heart to you, and with a calm manner, no yelling, no anger, you sit here and tell me like it is, dealing with your own demons, I am so lucky to have found you!" Claudia responded, "Look love, I don't like confrontations, I don't like the feeling of being angry, I don't fight over petty things, this situation can be worked out, with talking and understanding, all I ask is that you don't lie to me, I will never keep anything from you so please don't keep anything from me, so what you did was good, you trusted enough in me to open up, that's a sign to a great relationship." Still amazed by his girl Craig responds, "Well I have something else to tell you, today your gonna meet my mom, I've told her everything about you and she's very excited to meet you!" Claudia responds in disbelieve, "What! You didn't give me any warning that I was going to met your Mom, how old is she, my age? I don't even know what I'm going to tell her! I'm so embarrassed Craig, I really think you should of gave me some kind of warning, I don't think I'm ready to meet her!" With disappointment in his voice Craig responded, "Well actually my Mom's 42 and if you don't want to meet her I understand, but when you said you wanted to see how I lived that included my Mom Love, who do you think helps her out?" After all that Claudia felt selfish, "OK, if it means that much to you I'll met her." Claudia says with doubt, "I promise baby she is going to love you!" And with that said there was a knock at the door . . . .

Craig peeked out the window, "Um-mm it's not my Mom it's my Aunt Connie, my Mom's sister." Craig began to laugh. "Babe it's not funny, I feel so rocking the cradle right about now! How old is your aunt?" "40" Craig responded, then he opened the door. "Hi Mijo" his aunt said, "Where's your Mom?" "Hi Tia she stepped out for a little while but she'll be back soon. I want you to meet someone very special to me her name is Claudia." "Ahhh Claudia, buenos dias, it's so nice to finally meet you, we've heard so many nice things about you, I can honestly say that we've never seen Craig so happy, you must be a wonderful girl to do that to my nephew." "Craig is a very special guy and I feel blessed to have meet him." Claudia responds, "Well I'm gonna leave you two alone, Mijo tell your mom that I stopped by." "OK Tia" Craig responded and he walked her out. "See it wasn't that bad" "I guess not she seems very nice" Claudia says with a small chuckle.

It was 8 o'clock in the evening when Craigs Mom and step dad walked in the front door. Craig and Claudia were still sitting at the table laughing and talking, they could talk for hours. "This must be Claudia," Craigs Mom said with excitement. "Yes mom this is Claudia" Claudia stood up to shake her hand, and Craigs mother gave her a hug instead, giving her a firm hug, then she spoke. "Look Claudia, I've never seen my son so happy as I do with you. His last girlfriend gave him grief and never did she make him laugh or dress up. He walked around like he had a broom up his butt!" Claudia laughed, "For real Mija, he did, and now he walks around with a smile and sometimes I catch him humming a song that he says reminds him of you, so how can I dislike someone who brings joy to my son's heart? I can see me and you being good friends." Claudia felt a sense of relieve fill her body.

Craigs mom excused herself from the room, "I need to go to bed now, I have a early shift this morning, I go in at 3, so I'll leave you two alone, and Claudia feel free to stay the night, Craig says you live in Manhattan and it's getting late for you to take the subway, please stay, goodnight." "Thank you" Claudia responded, "I think I might take you up on that offer." "Ummm, yes please do love, rubbing her back all the way down her butt." And with all that said Claudia decided to stay the night.

Claudia wanted to take a shower and get refreshed so Craig excused himself so he could get Claudia the things she needed to shower, she sat in the dining room alone looking around the room. For a brief moment she began to laugh quietly so Craig couldn't hear her, she felt like a teenager staying over a friends house, a guy, imagine that! But in all reality she felt right at home, safe, loved, and no longer alone. Claudia was really surprised that meeting his Mom turned out so well, if that was her son bringing home a 40 year old Claudia would have pulled out nails, and lord knows what else, but it wasn't so it was easy to justify. She was happy and by what she saw so was Craig.

Claudia showered and put on one of Craig's T-shirts to sleep in. She walked out a little embarrassed but excited at the same time. It was awhile since Craig and Claudia's intimate moment so she needed to feel him again. As she crawled into bed Craig was already under the sheets waiting for her. At first it looked like he was asleep but as she pulled the covers over her body Craig turned around with a bolt of energy and swung his body around hers to hug her! Both of them laid there with a sense of security, Claudia never wanting to leave and Craig never wanting to let her go.

Claudia gently turned around to look at Craig in his eyes, the both of them starring like two love struck teenagers. Slowly Craig leaned into kiss Claudia kissing and pulling softly on her lips. As they both lay there with passion building up, Craig removed Claudia's T-shirt and with the silhouette of the night shining on her breast he began to devour them, kissing them gently, running his tongue around her nipples. Claudia's body clinched with excitement as she could feel the heat of his body, she turned over and wrapped her legs around his thighs slowly feeling his penetration as she slowly slid all the way down on him. She started to sway her hips back and forth slowly, she could hear Craig moan with every movement of her body, together they swayed, there bodies glistening with sweet sweat. Claudia tightened her muscles with each thrush. Craig lifted Claudia and lay-ed her on her back then he slowly penetrated her. She could feel his manly hood all through her body that a tear rushed down her cheek. All night the two of them lusted for each other and enjoyed the pleasures that man and woman had to offer. As the morning sun set, Craig and Claudia lay-ed there peacefully sleeping entwined in each others bodies with not a care in the world.

As the sun crept up that morning Claudia slowly opened her eyes, quenching with the light. "Oh my God, what time it it!" Claudia yelled. "It's 8:00am love, what's wrong?" Craig responds surprisingly, "I'm late for work, really late, by the time I ride the subway it will be 11:00 or so, I never do this!" Claudia never woke up with sunlight hitting her eyes, it was always dark when her alarm goes off, so this was way out of her element. "Look love I have an idea, why don't the both of us call in and spend the day together?" Craig responds with excitement, "Call in? Are you crazy, I have a million and one things to get ready, I don't have time to waste!" Claudia responds aggitated. With that said Claudia's phone rang it was Lola.

"You know I'm beginning to wonder about you, where are you and how come your not at work?" Claudia starred at Craig and realized how stupid she made him feel, so when Lola finished her sentenced Claudia responds, "Lola tell my boss that I won't be in today, tell him I feel sick but I'll be in tomorrow." There's a small silence on the phone, "You Liar! But you know I have your back, I'll take care of it for you, and by the way tell Craig I said Hi." Claudia laughed. As she hung up the phone Craig stood there still a little aggitated and hurt, "You didn't have to do that" "I know, but I rather be bored here with you than at work, so why don't you think of something exciting to do." Claudia responds sarcastically. "Can you handle a duty free environment, can you handle simple, that's what I want to know" Craig laughing as he challenges her. "I can be simple, I'll show you I'm not Miss Priss all the time, I can have a beer instead of Cosmos, heck, I'll even eat your fast food for lunch." Claudia giggling happy to oblige him. But Claudia had one issue, she continued to tell Craig, "There's one problem babe, I didn't bring any clothes." Craig responds "That's not a problem, I'll lend you some of my Moms, well come to think of it better not that was creepy just saying it, we will stop and buy you a outfit, tennis, a t-shirt and a pair of jeans." "Love I can't wait to see you dress casual, It will make me feel like we are on the same level!" Craig says with excitement! "Stop it! You always make me laugh Mr. Perez" So after a quick shop at the department store Claudia purchased what she thought was cute enough and they went back home to Craigs house to get ready and start there day.

"So what's on the agenda today, what could you possible have planned for me?" Claudia asked with excitement in her voice. Craig responds, "You can't laugh Love, but I wanted to go window

shopping, you know look at all the knew stuff for house decorating."
Claudia could not believe her ears! She was always up for shopping,
but never in her wildest dreams did she think that this macho man
had a soft side to him, of course she wanted to window shop, what
girl wouldn't want to do that with her man. Claudia responds, "Babe
you don't know how sexy you sounded when you asked me that, of
course I want to go window shopping with you, this way the girls
can see me with you and get jealous." Craigs faced turned RED!
"Love stop it, your making me blush and stutter I forgot what I
wanted to say!" So with that said they walked out the door to start
there adventure.

Claudia was so excited to see what Craig thought was window
shopping and Craig was a little nervous, he always felt the pressure
when it came to Claudia, to him she was so perfect and refined
that he didn't want to corrupt her with his ideas of fun, she was to
sophisticated for that or so he thought.

Chapter 6

Craig and Claudia proceeded down the street when Claudia saw a taxi, she started to flag it down when Craig yelled, "What do you think your doing?" Claudia responds with a strange look on her face, "What do you mean what am I doing, I'm calling a taxi so we can window shop." Still with a surprise look in her eyes. "How can you window shop when your flying by in a taxi? Explain that to me." Craig responds with a chuckle in his voice. Claudia looks over to him with a big smile, "I guess you have a point there, I'll give you one free get out of jail pass, besides the walk will do me some good, I need to lose some weight." Craig responds with a serious voice, "What do you mean lose weight, there's nothing wrong with you, I love you just the way you are! Do you like the way you look?" Claudia a bit puzzled but still responds, "Of course I do! Confidence is what makes a girl sexy, I think." Craig continues with his point, "See so if you are happy with yourself and I most definitely am happy with you why change, don't fix it if it ain't broke." Claudia begins to laugh . . . "OK for some strange reason that made sense, and all from a taxi ride, Craig you are some piece of work, but I'm glad. OK lets walk and do things your way." So with a big smile on both there face they continued to walk.

As they walked Claudia asked Craig, "Where's Macy's and a Prada store?" Craig looking at Claudia with that puzzled look in his face again. "Love we are in the Bronx not Manhattan, so let me take you somewhere that comes close, can you handle it?" "Funny" Claudia responds, "It was just a question. "Hey look at those purses in the window, that ones really cute can we look?" Claudia ask with excitement, "Of course love, let's see" Craig anticipating her reaction. "This purse is adorable! It's pink and just the right size and it's only 30 dollars can you believe it!" Claudia responds with sure excitement. "Well look at that" Craig responds sarcastically, "30 dollars, who would of know that kind of thing existed." Claudia laughs, "Can you show me more." Craig responds, "There's this store I want to take you to that I think your gonna like, it's right around the corner, let's hurry!" Claudia always loved to shop but today it felt so special she was doing it with someone who shared her interest and that meant so much to her, in her mind she was hoping that he was the one and at that moment she knew he was.

As Craig and Claudia walked two more blocks they came across this store that reminded Claudia of home, it was called Dream Home for Less and in this store were wall to wall items for your home. It had pictures, shelves, curtains, anything that had to do with your home at a reasonable price. Claudia got lost and caught up with the excitement! She could be in there for hours, Craig himself got caught up in the excitement the two of them were like children in a candy store and both of them enjoying the time they were spending with each other. After a while Craig started to feel hungry he turned and asked Claudia if she wanted to get a bite to eat, Claudia responded, "What do you feel like eating, Steak, Fish and Shrimp . . . ." "Whoa, wait a minute there" Craig stops her before she can go on, "I was thinking more like a dollar menu, or a hotdog from a hotdog stand, remember this is my date." Claudia sighed and agreed to his terms, "OK, whatever you want is fine with me." Craig responds with laughter in his voice, "You don't sound to excited but that's OK I'll take it!"

The two of them started to walk and came across this hotdog stand, "Wait!" Claudia says with excitement, "Let's eat hotdogs" "Are you sure" Craig responds "they are real hotdogs" "Funny" Claudia responds sarcastically "Let me have two hotdogs with the works, two bags of chips and one large coke" Craig tells the hotdog guy. "That will be $8.50" he responds, "See love, $8.50" "Wow you have skills" Claudia responds then they both began to laugh. They came across a bench at the end of the block and sat down to eat. It was one of the most romantic times Claudia had ever spent with a man and she loved every moment of it.

As the sun began to set Claudia tells Craig that she really needs to get back home. "Love I really need to get back to work tomorrow and it's getting late." Craig looks at her with a sad look in his eyes, "I know love it's just that it's hard to let you go each and every time I see you, but I understand." "I'll call you when I get home OK." Claudia responding with a sad tone in her voice.

Craig walks Claudia to the subway and realizes it will take her forever to get home so he calls a taxi and pays for it, Claudia still in disbelief that someone that wonderful exist leans over and gives him a passionate kiss before entering the taxi, "I love you Claudia" Craig whispers to her, "I love you too" Claudia responds with a lump in her throat, and with that the taxi drove away heading back to her destination. On the ride home Claudia sat back into her seat and thought about Craig the whole way home, his smile, his sense of humor, his cute facial expressions, the way he looked at here gave her goosebumps. This couldn't be happening to her she thought, a young man in love with her a older woman but in reality when Claudia spends time with him age isn't even a issue, she doesn't feel any older or does he act any younger, they are just a couple happy together loving each others company, at this moment Claudia feels grateful that she is no longer alone . . . .

The taxi finally pulled up to Claudia's apartment and she was happy to be home only because she was exhausted and needed to sleep. It became a habit that every time Claudia and Craig left each others presence they made it a point to call each other when either one of them got home, so Claudia called Craig and as soon as she hung up she fell fast asleep.

As always Claudia's alarm went off like it did every morning and Claudia woke anxious to get back to work, even though it was one day that she missed, it felt like a eternity and she knew that when she arrived at work it was going to be ciaos. Claudia was putting on her last minute accessories when her phone rang, it was Craig, "Hey" Claudia hears Crag's sexy voice, "Hey" Claudia responds with excitement. "Have you left for work yet" Craig ask with curiosity. "Just getting ready to walk out the door, why do you ask?" Claudia responds curious herself. "No reason just need a visual so I can start my day, what are you wearing love?" Claudia smirking responds, "We'll what would you like to see me in?" "Nothing"

Craig laughing. "Yeah I bet you would, as a matter of fact I'm keeping it professional with a little bit of sex appeal baby, you know how I am" Claudia responding confidentially, Craig with excitement in his voice responds, "Yes baby I know how you are and I Love it! I still ask myself what you see in me, but hey I'm not complaining because I have the sexiest girlfriend in New York!" Claudia's face with a smile from ear to ear responds "Well I'm pretty lucky myself, I have a diamond in the rough, a rare masterpiece that I myself am happy to keep." With those words said both Craig and Claudia hung up the phone happy to start there day.

Claudia arrived at work anxious to start her day when Lola with a agitated look on her face stops her, "What the hell do you think your doing?" Claudia calmly responds, "Going to work" Lola without any hesitance continues, "Well rumor is that you are starting to slack on your designs and corporate office is getting a little worried, they are talking about reviewing your designs!" Claudia standing with a long silence finally responds, "Lola I'm glad that your looking out for me, but there was one thing you said that is a key word to this, RUMOR, so I suggest you do like me and don't worry about it, I'm a big girl and I can handle it, besides it was one day that I missed, you would of thought I was out for months but I expected this, so I'm ready to handle whatever they have to put out, don't worry girl I'll be OK." You can hear the anxiety in Lola's voice when she responds, "You've worked so hard to get where you are and I don't want to see you lose everything for some boy toy, don't get me wrong Craig is a great guy but where can this relationship possibly be headed? Your a successful designer and he just looks cute at a corporate dinner." Claudia could feel the heat rush through her face, "Let me tell you something Lola not that it's any of your business but Craig is not a phase I'm going through and whether you believe it or not we are in a relationship! Granted I don't know where this is headed but then again that's with any relationship young or old, so I suggest that if you want to continue to be my friend you get your head out of your ass and accept the fact that I am with a younger man who happens to be very attracted to me that he puts it to me so good that my orgasms are not only multiple but so intense that even your momma would be proud! So if you would excuse me, I need to get to work, have a nice day" Lola stood there speechless as Claudia walked away, even though she really wanted to knock the living hell out of Lola, Claudia walked away with dignity and grace because that's how she carried herself.

Claudia found herself very busy and contrary to what Lola said everything seemed to be back to normal, no complaints about her work and as a matter of fact a new shipment was getting ready to be sent out. Sadly what Lola told Claudia that morning did stick in the back of her mind and it made for a gloomy day. Claudia began to wonder if Craig really was a mistake, what was his real motive for wanting to be with her. Claudia tried really hard to forget all that nonsense but it was already implanted in her head something that she dreaded. Claudia arrived at home at 8:00pm that evening from work and to her surprise Craig was sitting on the front stairs waiting for her. "Love what are you doing, why didn't you call me to let me know you were coming, I wouldn't of worked so late?" Craig a little agitated responded "I wanted to surprise my baby with dinner, but you seem tired love so maybe I should come back another night." Claudia looking sad responds, "Don't be silly come in, I'm glad your here with me baby, you have no idea what that does for me." "Really?" Craig responds "I'm glad I make you happy, that's all I want."

Claudia walks into her apartment with Craig following her right in, before she could put her things down, Craig em-brasses her and gives her a long passionate kiss. Claudia could feel her arms and legs turn into jello as he presses his lips against hers, melting away any negative thought that she had. As they opened there eyes Craig looks into Claudia's and ask "Is everything alright Love, you look sad, something I haven't seen in you." Claudia standing in disbelieve that he could read her already responds, "Actually it's nothing, well it's a little something but nothing to worry about." Craig looking at her confused, "OK now your not making any sense, so go put your things up, get comfortable, and get ready to eat, I ordered pizza for us and the delivery guy should be here soon so get relaxed and we will talk during dinner, does that sound good to you?" Mesmerized by him Claudia responds, "It's sounds great." With that said the doorbell rang.

Claudia walked to the room to change while Craig opened the door ready to pay for the pizza, Claudia hears a familiar voice and with a stunned look on her face walks to the front door. "Do you know a pizza guy named Sammy?," Craig asked Claudia with anger in his voice. "No I don't know a pizza guy named Sammy but I went out with a guy name Sammy a couple of times back in Texas right before I came to New York, why do you ask?" Claudia responds. "Well apparently he's kidnapped the pizza guy and came down to look for you, he's at the door with the pizza in his hand and says he's not moving till you talk to him. Claudia if there's something your not telling me now's the time to come clean because my angers rising and I'm getting ready to go knock the living crap out of this guy!" Claudia responds in disbelief, "Craig NO, look I don't have anything to do with him, we parted peacefully, well at least I thought we did, and I have no feelings for him at all, none, so in front of you I will tell him to leave and not come back, I don't want any part of him!" Craig takes a deep breath and responds, "Look Love I'm sorry if I'm coming off strong, but your what I've been waiting for all my life! So when a guy pops up on your doorstep I'm gonna freak out a little. So let me tell you what I'm gonna do, I'm gonna wait in the room and give you your space to talk to him, when your done you call me, I trust you Claudia so I'll be here waiting." Claudia's eyes began to water, "Your so wonderful Craig, thank you," So with that Claudia stood up and gave Craig a kiss on the forehead and walked to the door to greet Sammy.

Before Sammy could say a word Claudia began to talk "Look first of all before you even speak let me tell you something, I don't appreciate you coming down un announced to my house looking for trouble! What your doing is not tolerated or welcomed, as you can see I'm with someone so whatever it is you have to say, say it in five because after that you don't get a chance to speak again!" Sammy looks at her with a smirk, "Damn girl nice to see you too, I'm here on business so I decided to stop by and see how my Momma's doing, that's all, didn't mean to cause an up roar with your insecure boyfriend, oh yeah and by the way tell him the pizza's on me." Sammy laughs. Claudia answers with frustration, "Look he's far from being insecure, he just doesn't get off to arrogant idiots like you, who think there god's gift to women, besides he's better than that. How did you find me Sammy?" "It's not hard Ma" Sammy replied, "All you have to do is know how to pay the right people," Sammy laughs. Claudia responds agitated, "Look first of all I'm not your Ma so you really need to stop calling me that, and second, there's nothing left to say Sammy, whatever your looking for it's not me.

We both want different things and I'm happy with my life now so please just go and we'll take this as a nice gesture of hello, so please don't come back, I don't want any problems." Sammy stands there silent for a second, reaches into his pocket and pulls out a cigar, "Do you mind?" Sammy asks, "Yes I do because it prolongs your stay, so don't and leave already." Claudia responds. Sammy continues to speak, "Look Claudia I know I screwed up but I have a proposition for you, just listen to what I have to say then I'm gone, your life will never be the same again and you'll never have to work again in your life!" Claudia responds with a cold response, "Well it looks like your five minutes are way up, and as far as your proposition I'm not up for sale, I guess you haven't changed, so with that I'm ending this conversation so don't bother coming around here anymore I have nothing for you." Calmly, Claudia turned around and walked up the stairs back into her apartment. As she locked the door she glanced outside to see if Sammy left, he stood there, lighted his cigar then walked off with a grin of trouble. Claudia took a deep breathe and headed to the room to see Craig, as she opened the door Craig-ed layed there asleep, on her bed, looking like a troubled youngster, she couldn't help but to smile. It kinda made her feel special in a weird kind of way. She crawled into bed slowly and hugged him, as he felt her arms lay across him he let out a sigh, "I love you Claudia" Craig whispers to Claudia, "I love you too" And with that both of them lost there appetite, forgot about the pizza and went to sleep.

Chapter 7

It was 3 in the morning when Craig woke up, the sound of the rain hitting the window and the lightning brighting up the room is what woke him. He turned around to look at Claudia sound a sleep, she woke up because she could feel his breath on her face with one eye peaking open she caught him laughing. "What's so funny so early in the morning Love? Did I do something that I don't care to hear about?" Claudia ask with uncertainty, Craig responds "No love actually it's your hair, it's so funny to see you asleep because your hair sticks up like, hmmmm how can I describe it? Like you stuck your finger in a socket!" With embarrassement Claudia laughs, "Haha, see I told you I'm not perfect, It's the wax I put in my hair for the texture, now I'm gonna have to find something else." "No Love!" Craig responds, "I like your hair that way you look funny but cute, don't change it, I'm just playing with you." With that said they both laughed and tried to go back to sleep. 4 o'clock came when

Claudia feel asleep, before you know it her alarm went off and it was time for her to wake up for work.

Claudia got out of bed as always for her daily ritual only this time she had Craig there beside her. Craig himself had to wake up early because he had a early run. The both of them got dressed and Claudia drank her cup of coffee as Craig drank a Coke. The two of them were so different yet so right for each other. "I could get use to this Love" Craig tells Claudia with excitement, "What do you mean" Claudia responds, "I mean waking up with you every morning, going to work, you know the whole living together thing, It's nice to have someone around to keep you company don't you think?" Claudia hesitated to answer, "Ummm yes I think it would be interesting to share your life with someone" "Interesting, that's a weird way to put it" Craig responds comfused. With that said the conversation died out and both of them gave each other a kiss and darted out the door there seperate ways to start there day.

It was a busy day for Claudia, her spring collection hit the roof! Everyone involved was so excited, her fashion line didn't make her rich it just made her comfortable, this line definitely was going to change her income status. Claudia got a phone call that the corporate boss wanted to meet her so Claudia was excited but nervous at the same time. See whenever corporate wanted to meet with you it meant either you were on your way to success or you were on your way out the door, hopefully it was a positive thing for Claudia. Everyone in the office was talking that morning about Claudia's meeting with the big boss which didn't make it a easy day for Claudia, it made her nervous and anxious to know what was going to happen, but with a positive attitude Claudia continued on with her day.

It was 4 o'clock when they finally called Claudia in for her big meeting, Claudia could feel her hands sweating and her legs started to feel like jello. All she could think about was her days in Texas and her husband who died, what would he say about her now? Right before she entered the room her cell phone rang, it was her Mom, "Mija" Claudia heard with a low voice, "It's Mom"

"Mom" Claudia responded with excitement, "You always know when to call me, how do you do that?" Claudia's mom responds with a chuckle, "It's mothers intuition, which I'm hoping you will find out one of these days if you would give yourself the opportunity to find a man" Claudia's mom still chuckling as she speaks, "Look mom I have a very important meeting I'm attending right now but as soon as I'm done I promise I'll call you right back." "Aye Mija pos dime algo, call me back when you have a chance," and with that they both hung up the phone.

Claudia took one deep breath before she entered the room, little did Claudia's mom know the confidence she gave Claudia just by hearing her mother's voice, with that Claudia was ready to embrace whatever was coming her way. As she strutted right in, the two big double doors closed right behind her, followed by silence, her meeting was about to begin.

Sitting at the head of the table was a heavy set Caucasian man Mr. Holland, clean cut wearing a blue pinned stripped suit with a yolk yellow collared shirt, not something Claudia would of personally picked out but when your a big time executive she figured they could wear whatever they wanted. And sitting to the left of him was Ms. Ying a very petite woman with a very keen sight for style, she came off as a quite lady but when it came down to business quite she was not. There was one other woman and two other men that Claudia had never seen before so she was starting to feel the pressure.

"Sit down, Claudia" Mr. Holland said with a smile, "You seem to be a bit nervous and I could understand why, but there is no need I promise you that. This is my team of consultants, as you know this is Ms. Ying and to the right of her it's Mr. Sanches and Ms. Dewitt. Sitting across is Mr. Fuentes" Claudia with a big smile introduced herself and continued to listen. Mr. Holland continued to speak,

"I'm very very impressed with your line of clothing that you've put out this spring and I must say being a husky guy myself I like the way that you've portrayed the heavier side of American woman to be and that is beautiful and sexy. Seeing it through your eyes of fashion is amazing! You have made what America considers plus size woman to be sexy in any size and that for us is profitable. Do you understand what were trying to say?" Claudia sat there listening, understanding but yet a little confused, responded, "Either your calling me in to give me positive recognition or your offering me a business proposal and I'm leaning towards my second guess." Everyone in the room chuckled, Mr. Holland responds, "Why yes my dear your right! Not only do you have good fashion sense you have a good sense of humor, but yes we are offering you a business proposal. We know you have your fashion line but what we want to do is expand your line worldwide. The United States might be the country with obesity on the rise but Germany has what we like to say big bone woman. Full figured woman are all over the globe not just America so why not make every woman feel confident about herself?" Claudia sat there quite and in disbelieve, Mr. Sanches began to speak, "Look Claudia I know this is a lot for you to handle right now, this is just the tip of the iceberg. Your gonna have to travel more and create more as time progresses, but we know that you can do it that's why we are here. Now your salary is going to be more than what you imagined just for putting your line out there, but if it takes off like we know it will the royalties will put you in the millionaire bracket and that I know is what you work for we will be here to guide you and make sure you get paid what you are worth. We have a contract that will guarantee you $800,000 starting salary and the rest is up to you." Claudia was speechless, she sat there quite which seemed like an eternity but was only a couple of minutes, took a deep breath and then began to speak, "This has always been my dream to design clothes and I was comfortable doing just what I'm doing now, pay and all, but your right it's time for me to venture out to big and better things and this is going to be a opportunity of a lifetime, so I definitely am going to take this offer and run with it!" Everyone in the room began to clap! Mr. Holland spoke, "Claudia you've made a good decision and I promise you that we are going to the top with this, I promise you!" Mr. Holland called for a bottle of the best champagne to celebrate and that they did.

As soon as the meeting and celebrating were over Claudia wanted to call Craig but she knew the first person she had to call was her mother, so that's what she did. As she was dialing the numbers all she could think about was growing up and the struggles her parents had just so she and her sisters could have a good life. She thought about her deceased husband and she thought about Craig. She had gone so deep into thought that she heard her moms voice faintly "Hello, hello, Mija, Claudia?" "Oh momma, hello it's me Claudia, I'm sorry I got lost in thought and I forgot that I called you." "Is everything OK," Claudia's mom responded, "Never better" Claudia answers. "I just got out of the meeting with the big bosses and your never gonna guess Momma, they offered me $800,000 for my line of clothes plus royalties! Mom this is more than I could ever imagine." There was a long stretch of silence and with a broken voice her mother responded, "Ay Claudia I am so proud of you, I always knew this day would be coming, I just wish your dad was here to share your happiness." "Momma are you crying?" Claudia responds, "Yes my love but they are tears of happiness, your sisters are going to be so proud of you, so proud." "Mom I want you to come down to New York with Beatrice and Yoli I'll pay all the expenses, I just want family here even if it's just for a little while. I have something special that I want to share with you and my sisters." Claudia's mom responds, "You mean there's more good news? Why can't you just say it know?" Claudia responds excitedly, "No mom I think it's better in person, so get back to me and let me know what my sisters say, I have to hang up now but I'll keep in touch, I love you." And with that they hung up.

For some reason Claudia was a bit nervous to tell Craig about the wonderful business venture she was about to start. He never came across as a jealous person but still she was hesitant. She figured maybe she was putting in to much into it. So when she got home she was going to invite him over and tell him, it was going to change both there lives and for the better, so Claudia thought.

As she walked back to her office everyone stood up and began to clap, even Lola. As she made that stretch across the hallway Claudia began to feel a lump in her throat and tears fill her eyes. As she continued to walk one of her coworkers stopped her, and spoke, "Do you know what you've done for the Hispanic Community? You've added one more name to many that have succeeded and that put's all Hispanics on the map, you've made a little Hispanic girl or boys dream closer to reality." Claudia never felt so accomplished and happy in her life. She had never seen it in that point of view and she was happy that someone did and pointed it out to her. At that moment she felt truly blessed . . .

Claudia was getting ready to call it a day when her office phone rang, it was Craig, "Hello, Babylove" Craig speaks, "Hey Baby, how are you?" Claudia responds, "I'm good, I haven't heard from you so I was beginning to worry, are you ok?" Claudia responds with hesitation, she couldn't believe she was having such a hard time telling Craig, "Yes baby I'm good, hey I was wondering if you had a chance if you could stop by tomorrow, I would like to see you." "I could stop by tonight, I don't have anywhere to go if that's ok with you." Craig responds, "Ummm sure that sound good, so tonight it is." Claudia says her goodbyes and when she hangs up her stomach begins to girgle, why is she having a hard time with this, she should be happy to share this with Craig but for some reason she's reluctant and doubt begins to settle . . . .

Claudia's taxi ride home was filled with all kinds of excitement, doubt and worries. How was all this going to come together? So many things to iron out: designs, shippings, retail, so many things but her main concern was the love of her life, Craig. Maybe she was making more of this than it was, as her taxi drove up to her door there he was standing at the stairs looking handsome as ever smiling as she got out of the car. "Hello my love how are you tonight? You look lovely as ever." Craig responds with happiness in his voice, "I'm just fine Craig, you always know how to put a smile on my face." "Craig? That's unusual we haven't called each other by our first names scince we've gotten serious, are you sure your ok?" Craig responds with concern. "As a matter of fact never better, I didn't know calling each other by our first names was a crime, be sure to check in next time

I go there!" Claudia annoyed. Craig responds confused, "Ok maybe I missed something, do we need to start over, did I say something to upset you? Because I don't feel I did." Craig a little annoyed himself. As Claudia turned to look at Craig her eyes began to fill with tears as she began to speak, "Oh Love, I'm sorry, sit her on the steps with me because I need to talk to you and I don't think I can wait till we get inside. Something very wonderful happened to me today and I'm so overwhelmed by it all that I'm just having a difficult time absorbing it, it's making me act out baby, I just don't know how to feel." Craig sitting listening his heart ponding, Claudia continues, "Today Mr Holland, one of the big time bosses called me in for a special meeting, which at first I had no idea what was going on, he continue to tell me that they where very interested in my clothing line, and to make a long story short, they offered me $800,000 to start with a market value of over a million dollars with royalties, what I'm trying to say my love is that I took the offer and I begin immediately! I just don't know how to feel right now, this is a dream come true for me you know?" Craig sat there with a strange look on his face which Claudia had a hard time figuring out, he began to speak. "Oh my God Baby that is so wonderful and so overwhelming to hear, My Lady is a superstar! How can anybody top that? You are doing what you always wanted to do, your dreams and prayers have finally been answered, what more can a wonderful woman like you ask for, you so deserve every wonderful moment!" Claudia sat there with so much emotion, tears running down her face, "Oh Love I'm so happy to hear that, for a minute I thought . . . . well forget what I thought, I'm just happy!" Craig stood up and began to walk to the door, "Are we going inside? The night mist is beginning to get to me." "Sure" Claudia responds. "You know Baby, I think I'm gonna go ahead and call it a night, I'm not feeling to good, I'll give you a call in the morning, is that ok with you?" Claudia stood there stunned but what could she say, "Ummm ok, I can take care of you, you know, you don't have to leave." Craig responds, "I know but I just want to go, don't worry I'll call you tomorrow." With that said Craig kisses Claudia on the forehead and walks away. Claudia stood there with sadness in her heart because at that moment she felt like she was never going to see him again . . . .

Chapter 8

Morning came and as excited as Claudia should have been, she was not. She lay there as her alarm clock rang and all she could think about was Craig. She thought about calling him that morning but didn't she really needed to concentrate on her line of clothing and where to begin, so without anymore hesitation she jumped out of bed and got ready for work.

As Claudia walked into the office she could feel the excitement and energy that everyone was carrying. "Good morning, Ms." one of the workers said with enthusiasm, Claudia smiled and thought "Wow funny I've been through this office so many times and that young lady not once wished me a good morning, this is going to be interesting to see how people change." Claudia just gave a big smile as she entered her office. As she was putting her things away and getting ready for her day a tall handsome man, medium built, with dark hair and blue eyes entered right behind her, "Yes can I help you?" Claudia looks at him puzzled, "The question is can I help you? My name is Tony Mitchel and I've been assigned as your new secretary, if that's OK with you?" "Ahhhh sure that's fine with me but I didn't know I was getting a secretary, male for that matter." Claudia giggles and continues to speak, "Let's start by holding all my calls because it's gonna be a very busy day, and if you don't mind can I just call you Tony, you can call me Claudia because we are going to be seeing a lot of each other these next couple of months and when we have a chance we will take a lunch so we can get to know each other how does that sound?" Tony responds with a smile, "OK Ms, I mean Claudia that sounds like a good way to start the day, someone in the office hinted to me that you like espresso in the morning so here you go, got it nice and fresh for you, I'm gonna be getting your agenda ready for you so if you will excuse me . . ." "Sure of course" Claudia smiles and Tony leaves to start his day. Just as Claudia's getting ready to go through her papers Mr. Holland walks in. "Good morning Ms. Cruze how's it going for your first big day as top fashion designer?" "A little overwhelming but exciting to say the least, what do we owe for this wonderful presence today Sir?" "OK now young lady, no need for flattery you have already won my vote." The both stood there and laughed as Mr. Holland continued, "Before you get started with your agenda I wanted to be the first to show you your knew place of employment" Claudia stood there with a worried look on her face, "You cannot be a top fashion designer without a top notch office, so if you could get Tony to gather your things let me walk you down to your new office, I'm sure you will find it quite comfortable to your liking." Claudia excited grabbed her purse and darted out right behind Mr. Holland. As the two continued to walk Claudia's heart began to pound, they where walking through the halls of some of the most important people in this building and as they got closer to there destination right there on the door was a name plate with Ms. Claudia Cruz Top Fashion Designer, Claudia's eyes began to tear she finally reached her dream she had arrived it was now time for her to shine and show the world what she was made of.

Claudia walked in and as you entered the room there was a big sitting area with leather sofas and a beautiful round iron table to the left was a espresso machine, and mini bar. To the right was a beautiful shelf with modern art. On the shelf was a picture of Claudia's Mom and Dad in a beautiful cream colored picture frame. In that moment as Claudia stared into the picture she got caught in thought, how happy her Dad would have been if he was alive right now and how proud her Mom is of her now. Claudia urn ed for her families presence so with that she had Tony call and book her Mom and sisters flights it was time for some family love.

Mr. Holland excused himself for the day and Claudia continued to get settled in, it was something she had not anticipated but was excited to do. As twelve o'clock came near Claudia called Tony into the room, "Hey Tony I don't know about you, but I'm getting hungry, how about you calling in some Chinese and we can sit here in my new office and break it in, you know get aquinted at the same time." Tony responds, "Sounds good to me, I'll call it in and you can continue doing what your doing, oh by the way Chicken Chop Suey right?" Claudia impressed, responds, "Hey it looks like you've done your homework on me, I like that, yes Chop Suey it is." Tony leaves with a smile on his face.

As the morning started to die down a bit Claudia sat down behind her new desk and it hit her, Craig had not called her all morning. Claudia began to get chocked up a new chapter in her life and no man to share it with, not any man but the love of her life. It was not fair, how can she apologize for something she worked so hard for, she was not going to call him. Claudia figured when he was ready he would call her. Just then Tony walked in with lunch.

Tony and Claudia sat sprawled out on the floor, Tony speaks, "You know I would of never thought I'd be having so much fun on my first day," Claudia responds amused, "Don't get to excited we will be very busy and I do expect a lot from you Tony, I just didn't want you to feel overwhelmed on your first day being I had no idea I was getting a Assistant." Tony responds with his guard up, "No, no, I'm sorry I didn't mean to come off strong like that . . . ." "Don't worry about it, you didn't tell me about yourself Tony and what made you pick this profession?" Claudia waiting anxiously for a response. "Well I graduated from the University of Texas in Austin," "Oh my God your a Texan!" Claudia responds excited. "Yes mame born and raised in Dalllas, I came down with my fiance for a job in business but found it hard to get a job so Mr. Holland and my fiance's Mom use to go to school together so he promised me a job with a top notch fashion designer, so I thought this ought to be interesting so I took it, what do I have to lose? So here I am working for you, Ms. Top notch fashion designer." Both of them laughed. "So you have a fiance that's wonderful, so when is the big day, if you don't mind me asking?" Tony continues, "I'm not to sure, Cindy that's my fiance, wants a winter wedding, it really doesn't matter to me I just want time to be settled actually, then I will be happy." Claudia responds, "Yes New York is a tough place to get settled in everything is rush, rush, and so expensive but it is a nice place to live especially in the winter time. I'm very flexible so whatever time you need to help the Mrs. to be just let me know." "Wow, thank you I'm sure Cindy would like that." Tony responds surprisingly, he continues, "So what about you Claudia, if you don't mind me asking, anyone special in your life?" Claudia silent for a moment responds, "As a matter of fact yes, his name is Craig, hes wonderful, and I feel very lucky to have him in my life, but right now with all the big changes I feel like he doesn't want to be part of it . . . . haven't heard from him since I've given him the news, I don't know maybe he's just giving me time to settle in." Tony responds, "Yes I'm sure it's just that, well Claudia I need to do my job so I need to inform you that you have a 2:00 meeting with some people from Essence magazine they want to do a photo shoot with some plus models in your clothing line so freshen up and the car will be waiting downstairs to pick us up." Claudia a bit confused responds, "Fashion shoot, I don't even know what they are looking for, what do they want?" Tony continues, "Don't worry, I took care of that for you all you have to do is show up and give orders, how easy is that? Would love to be in your shoes Ms. Claudia!" Claudia laughs and continues, "Well then that was easy so let's go Tony and get this started, I feel like it's gonna be a wonderful evening after all." With that said the both of them head downstairs to the car, with a sh-offer waiting to take them to there destination.

In the car ride to the shoot all Claudia could think about was Craig, it was getting her mad the more she thought about the situation. How can she be sorry for something she worked hard for all her life, and why should he be upset if that was the case? She decided that from that moment she was going to concentrate on her work and if he wanted to see her he knew where to find her, if it where that easy. By this time Claudia grew lioness and not anyone was going to get in her way even if it was the love of her life.

It was 3:30 when they arrived to the shoot, this was Claudias first time getting models ready for a fashion shoot she imagined it was easier than a fashion show but who knows she was about to find out. When she walked in she was greeted by the photographers then the coordinator, "Hi my name is Jesse and I'm from Essense, I'm really pleased to be working with these plus size models and your clothing line is extrodinary! America is coming around and excepting the fact that America is big but also beautiful, so with that said let's get started." Claudia was excited! She gathered her models and put ensambles together that she hadn't done before and it worked out great, the shoot took 6 hours but worth every minute. The models looked gorgeous and Claudia couldn't be any happier with how they looked, now they had to wait for the critics when the magazine comes out next month in June. One thing out of many that they had going on.

There was one thing that constantly ran thru her mind and it was Craig, her heart broke everytime she thought of him and how he hadn't tried to get in contact with her, how can being successful be a bad thing that it would ruin a relationship? Claudia sat there in a daze trying to justify his actions then it hit her, she wasn't. How can she justify being successful, it's something she worked hard for all her life but she also thought about Craig and his struggles and it began to make sense to her, she couldn't be mad at him she knew that he felt like a nobody and that in his mind he couldn't take care of her like he knew she deserved and anyways it was something she did by herself, she was the most independent woman he ever met, well that's what she remembers in a conversation they had.

As she sat there she decided that she wasn't going to beat herself up trying to figure it out, it is what it is and successful she was and she wasn't going to appologize to anyone for it, even Craig, so with that she decided to bury herself in her work and go day by day which is all that she could do.

As Claudia got her things together to call it a night Tony stumbles over to talk to her, "Well Claudia I would have to say that you did a wonderful job, I'm very impressed," "Thanks Tony, I appreciated that but really you don't have to kiss ass I already like you as my assistant" Both laughing, Tony continues "I have some exciting news that hopefully gets you out of your misery, don't think I didn't notice, with all this excitement I still see sadness, so with that your Mom and sisters will be her on Saturday on the 2:00 flight from Dallas so I have a limo set to ride them wherever you want them to go. I know you wanted them to stay with you but let's face it you did mention that your place was small so being the wonderful assistant that I am I booked a suite at the Sheraton with a spa appointment for all four of you, yes I know you don't have to thank me, I'm wonderful." As Claudia laughed she preceded to talk, "Are you finish filling your head with air, because if you are I want to say thank you, you are pretty wonderful but no raises yet for you mister maybe around your wedding . . . . hehehe And also since you mentioned my small apartment I think it's time to up grade remind me to look into some real estate looks like I'm going to broaden my living space." As they both called it a night, Claudia left back to her apartment excited to see her family it's something she really needed, some motherly love and tender loving care from her sisters she was excited . . . .

Chapter 9

Well Saturday morning arrived and Claudia was very excited, her Mom and sisters Beatrice and Yoli where coming in from Texas to see her, she could hardly wait. With all the excitement Claudia forgot that she had something to tell them and that something was Craig so how was she going to handle that? It was something that she would have to decide when the time comes meantime she had to get ready to meet them at the hotel, she decided that it would be fun to stay with them and catch up with stories about her nieces and nephews besides the thought of going back to a empty apartment wasn't to pleasing so she decided to join them.

As Claudia was packing her weekend bag the phone rang, her heart began to race hoping that it was Craig, she stumbled as she answered her phone, "Hello, hello?" an unfamiliar voice answered back, "Claudia?" "Yes" she responded, "Hey it's me Hank, how's it going" As she stood there her heart fell to the floor as she clenched her teeth and phone with disappointment, "Oh hi Hank, what can I help you with I'm kind of busy right now." he responded annoyed, "Sorry to bother you just wanted to know if you and Lola wanted to hang out for a drink or something, haven't seen you girls around for a while and I was hoping . . . ." Before he could finish his sentenced Claudia responds, "Don't mean to cut you short but my taxi's here, been really busy with my new position so I don't have time for anything really, thanks for thinking of us but we will have to pass, bye take care." And with that said Claudia hung up the phone. "Uuuugggggghhhhh" the frustration was building up inside of her all she wanted was to hear Craigs voice but she had to much pride to call him so she gathered herself together and called a taxi so she could go meet her family.

It was 2:30pm when she arrived at the hotel her families plane arrived at 2:00 but she wanted to be there to greet them and make sure everything was in place for them besides the New York rush would have them at the hotel around 3:30 so she had plenty of time. As she entered the room she was impressed, "Oh my God, I so owe Tony for this, this is beautiful" she said to herself. The room had a beautiful view of downtown Manhattan the sitting room had high ceilings with lighted crown molding, white sofas with beautiful chrome accents and gold pillows, there where fresh flowers everywhere so the room smelled fresh, it was a three bedroom suite with a huge bar and flat screen TV, there was a bottle of champagne and fresh strawberries ready to greet them this made Claudia very happy, the thought that she was able to do this for her family overwhelmed her and for a moment it healed the pain that she felt for Craig.

It was 3:30 on the dot when the front desk called on the intercom, "Ms. Cruse?" "Um-mmm Yesss" she responds impressed, "Your family arrived and I just sent them up, if you need anything just give me a buzz, my name is Kathy and I'll be yourpersonall assistant today," "thank you, I appreciated that" Claudia responded excited. She finished talking to the intercom when there was a knock at the door, Claudia ran to open it.

As she opened the door there was a enormous amount of screaming, Claudia couldn't help herself, she began to cry . . . .

The first person she hugged was her mother, and with a soft voice her mother spoke, "Ah my first born, it is so wonderful to see you, and how impressed we are, not expecting all this, I've missed you so much Mija, I love you" Claudia, choked up, responded, "Oh Mom you have no idea how wonderful it feels to have you hold me, I'm glad your here to share this experience with me even though it is only for a little while." As the two of them walked in the foyer, her sisters began to scream again, Beatrice speaks first "Wow sis look at you, you look wonderful and this place is nice let me tell you . . . ." The three of them laugh, Yoli speaks, "I knew that my big sister would one day make it big and wow, look at you!" Claudia responds happy, "There's so much going on and I will tell but first you guys need to get settled in and relax I know it's been a long morning, whatever you guys want to do is fine with me."

As Claudia helped her mother get settled in, the girls took a small tour around the room. Beatrice turns to speak to Yoli, "Did you look at the set up in the bar? How much do you think those tiny bottles cost?" Yoli laughs and responds, "Can you show a little class? I think our sister has it covered, don't be a lush." "Ha, ha" Beatrice responds.

Claudia calls them all to sit down so they can pop the champagne bottle for a toast. As Claudia begins to pop open the bottle her Mom begins to speak, "It gives me such a warm feeling of pride as I sit her with my 3 beautiful daughters, your Dad would be very proud of each and everyone of you. Claudia, I know it's been hard for you to be away from home, ever since you lost your husband you've buried yourself, your life, in your work, and I always worried about you, I didn't quite understand it but your Dad always told me to let you be, one day you would find yourself and as we sit here I see exactly what he meant and I worry no more because I see happiness and a sense of accomplishment that truly brings joy to my heart." As her mother spoke Claudia's eyes began to swell and for a moment could not speak a word but after she compelled herself she herself began to speak, "Mom it makes me so happy to hear that, I've been thru so much in my lifetime but you know what, I'm not bitter, I'm happy with the way my life's turning out, I can have anything I want, and everybody seems to appreciate my work so I'm good." Without further hesitation Beatrice begins to speak, "Hey so mom says you had something juicy to tell us, so do tell sis we've been trying to figure it out all the way over here, are you dating some famous guy? Is it John or Sylvester, oh it's that guy that comes out in that movie you love so much ummmm Sex in the City," Everyone laughs, Claudia shakes her head and responds, "No none of the above, but I did meet someone and I guess the juicy part about it is he's about half my age, well almost, he's 24" There was total silence for what seemed to be a eternity. Beatrice breaks the silence, "Damn sister that news is way better and juicer than any old famous person!" Everyone laughed but waited for there Mom to respond and she did, "Are you happy?" She asked, Claudia takes a deep breath and responds, "Very happy he brings shivers down my spine when he talks to me, he makes me laugh, he loves everything about me and he doesn't judge me, when we are together age doesn't seem to be a factor, we are just ourselves, and I love him . . ." With that said a tear ran down Claudia's face and Yoli spoke, "Hearing you and seeing your expression is enough for me sis, I can't wait to meet the kid, just kidding, I mean I can't wait to meet him," "That wasn't very nice" Beatrice responds, Yoli continues, "Oh get over it she's gonna have to get use to the jokes besides it beats us being against her then what?" Claudia's mom speaks, "Okay girls that's enough leave your sister alone, if that's what you want Mija then I agree with your sister, you glow when you talk about him so I'm excited to meet this young man." Claudia takes another deep breath, she didn't know what to say but before she knew it a lie leaked out from her lips, "He's out of town this weekend on business and he didn't know you guys where coming if not he would of made arrangements to stay but I promise that you guys will meet him next time.

With that said the four of them got changed into semi formal attire and got ready for a wonderful dinner at one of the top restaurants in Manhattan, it was something else Tony, Claudia's assistant had lined up for them, Claudia felt truly blessed.

The time that Claudia's family was there, she took them shopping, had a spa appointment, more food, and caught a play, by the last day of there visit they where all exhausted, it was Sunday night the day before they leave and they decided to stay in the hotel and rent a movie. Beatrice and Yoli decided to nap while Claudia stayed up to reminisce with her Momma it was something that she needed to fill the void she was feeling, nothing like family memories to take care of that.

"Do you remember the day I told you I was getting married" Claudia ask her mom with a look of sadness, "Yes I do, it was probably one of the most overwhelming days of mine and your father's life" Her mother responds, "Yes I was young wasn't I, But I thought I knew it all, I wonder what my life would have been like if he was still alive?" Claudia sits with a look of distant thought, Claudia's mom responds, "Honestly I don't think you would be where your at now, he was always so controlling and every time he said jump, you said how high." Claudia responds a bit agitated, "Oh mother!, that's not true . . . . Was I really like that?" Claudia looked confused, "Yes you did and it drove me and your father crazy, your father was sad for what happened to him because of you but deep down I think he found joy in the sense he was out of your life, it's not a nice thought but you remember how your father was and anyone that would hurt his girls there was hell to pay!" Claudia sat there surprised with her mothers response, "I never knew that Dad felt that way, funny thing is I did love him though, why I don't know because he was one of those macho men, but I loved him, I miss him sometimes." Claudia's mom responds, "So this new man in your life, do you love him?" Claudia sat there in a daze and hesitated before she answered, "I do love him, when we are together I don't feel any pressures from my work, my life or even from myself. He puts everything into prospective for me, and as far as our age difference there isn't any, he doesn't act any younger and I don't act any older we are just ourselves. The only thing that seems to be a issue is our jobs," Claudia's mom interrupts with a look of confusion, "Your jobs? How does that hurt your relationship?" Claudia continues to explain, "Well he's your average blue collar worker, which I don't have any problems with, in fact I think It's sexy to see him in a uniform and I'm a successful fashion designer, in his mind it's not working, he should be making as much money as me or more to support the finer things in life that I do for myself, so that cause's a problem." Claudia's mom responds, "but mija that shouldn't be a issue if your OK with it, are you OK with it?" Claudia answers annoyed and a raised voice, "OF COURSE WHY WOULDN'T IT BE!" Claudia's mom continues, "I didn't mean to upset you I'm just trying to understand, why would he feel that way if you haven't given any indication that it bothers you why would it bother him?" Claudia sat there lost in thought and silence, had she shown him that it bothered her without realizing it? Could she have sent out the wrong signal? It never bothered her but maybe subconsciously it did. At that moment Claudia was feeling worst than she had before, maybe his isolation from her was her fault only time could tell what was about to happen because he still hadn't contacted her. As Claudia and her mother finished there conversation, Beatrice and Lola came into the room from there nap. They popped in a movie, drank some wine, and vegged out the rest of the night. As the night continue they all fell asleep and Claudia felt secure with her family around her.

The next day Claudia rode with them to the airport, Claudia and her sisters hugged each other and tears ran down there face, Claudia's mom hugged her tight and blessed her, which is what most Catholics do for a sense of protection, Claudia was so glad to have spent those days with her family it was what she needed to continue on with her life, nothing like family love to put you back together. As they boarded there plane Claudia waved goodbye and headed back to reality.

Chapter 10

Claudia's heart felt a little empty after leaving her family, so to keep her mind off of things she started to bury herself in her work it always helped her to ease her pain and keep her mind occupied on things besides family and Craig. As she began to get closer to work she started thinking about her models, all her models where picked especially for her clothing line, so why not have her own personnal make up artist? As she sat there thinking Lola came to mind. Even though things where a bit distant between them, Claudia figured that Lola would be perfect for the job. So the first thing Claudia did when she arrived to work was give Lola a call.

The phone rang twice before Lola answered, "Hello" "Well hey stranger" Claudia replied, there was a short silence, "well it's finally nice to here from you scince about a year" Lola answers sarcastically, Claudia responds, "Very funny, you know I've been very busy with this new career venture of mine, besides I hear you've been pretty busy yourself with the new love in your life" there's a slight hesitation, Lola continues to speak, "Where did you here that nonsense?" Claudia laughs, "Uhuh you know you can't hide anything from me, just hope your happy that's all, I wanted to talk to you about something so I was wondering if you wanted to do lunch, it's business." Lola responds, "I can't do lunch today have a very busy schedule, why don't you just tell me now while you have me on the phone, who know's how long before I talk to you again . . . ." Claudia with a frown on her face responds, "Well this is not how I like to do business but scince it's you I guess I'll have to make an exception. Everything with my clothing line is going really well I just didn't know how much was involved with all this, I'm so use to just designing, few shows here and there and sending my clothes to department stores, but now that my line is venturing out, models, hair dresser, you know all that implies with it . . ." Lola interrupts, "Can you just get to the point your procrastinating?" Claudia frustated with Lola responds, "Look I wanted to know if you would like to work for me as my make up artist for my models, I have a good package to offer you with full benefits, I mean you don't have to say yes your not obligated to do so being we are friends and all, just thought you would like to try something different, you would be doing a lot of traveling and it's on the go all the time but you know . . ." Lola interrrupts, "So you want me, to work for you, traveling non stop on some occassions? Humm . . . ." there's silence between them, "What took you so damn long to ask? I've been so excited for you but at the same time I was a little upset, I was wondering why you hadn't included me? No phone call, no visits, I know your busy but I thought you would always be here, remember we are like sisters. But before I continue to babble on and on about this or that I would love to go work for you but I need to put my two weeks notice here before and square away some things, I'm so excited!!!" Claudia responds with excitement, "Well this is going to be interesting to see, I will have Tony call you in about two weeks with details" Lola interrrrupts, "Tony who's Tony?" Claudia responds, "Oh I'm sorry he's my assitant I don't take care of those things anymore, I'm to busy with other things, besides he's really wonderful your gonna like him, and by the way I'm house hunting so maybe you can take time and help me out, it would be nice having your input again!" They both laugh, Lola responds, "Ok well I need to get back to work talk to you soon and thank you my friend." Claudia closes the phone with a smile on her face, it's gonna be nice having someone she knows close by, working with her and keeping her grounded that's something Claudia looked forward too.

As she continued with work Tony walks into her office, "Hey Ms. Claudia how did your visit with your family go, hope you got some well needed rest." Claudia responds, "You know Tony I did get some well needed rest and I would like to thank you for all that you did, the room was beautiful and my Mom and sisters where very impressed and all because of you. That really wasn't necessary I don't expect you to take care of personnal matters but you did a wonderful job, I really appreciate it." Tony responds with a smile, "No problem, I actually enjoy things like that, here's your agenda for today, everything highlighted is of importance, everything else can wait till tomorrow, have conference room ready for you for your 10:00 meeting with Essence, so your business suit the one you like so much, is pressed ready to go hanging in your closet whenever you are, so see you in an hour." With that said Tony left the room.

Claudia sat there still in aw with everything, it still was a bit difficult to grasp all that was happening in her life, sometimes she didn't know if to laugh, cry, or scream, but with everything she was still greatful to be where she was with her career if only Craig was there to share it with her . . . .

Chapter 11

Craig lay there that Monday morning, numb and disgusted with himself. He wanted to call Claudia but could not get the strength to do so. He was so proud of her and her success but felt worthless in the process. How could anyone so successful want a nobody? In his mind that's what Craig felt, like a nobody. He left her with no reasons as to why he was acting like he was, he could not get the courage to look her in the face and explain his reasoning's for his behavior, that indeed he was proud of her but that it was himself that he was not happy with, instead he disappears out of her life, like a rain cloud teasing, then quietly disappearing away. Since the last day that he saw her, he has never been the same, his heart aches everyday that passes and with every day that passes the pain worsens.

Craigs intent was not to leave Claudia but what he wanted was to better himself and not with Claudia's help, he knew that if he stayed with her she would only want to help him and paying his way to success through her is not what he wanted or would allow so he felt he would have to cut ties with her and do this on his own, his only regret would be that she not be there when he was ready, but it was a risk he felt he had to take . . . .

Craig quit his job at the warehouse and decided to go to business school, his plan was to get educated with the business process and absorb enough knowledge to open up a business of his own, he was hoping that when all was said and done, Claudia would be just as proud of him as he was of her but time could only tell what life had in store, he just hoped that Claudia would love him enough to understand, as selfish as that might have sounded . . . .

As days, weeks, and months passed, Craig buried himself in the books and tried to keep as busy as possible, not one day went by that Craig didn't think about Claudia but the more he thought of her the more it pushed him to succeed, all he wanted was to be able to give her everything that she deserved and nothing less. Every now and then his Mom would pop in on him to check on him, the sadness and tiredness around his eyes worried her and thought that maybe sometimes he was taking this a bit to far, when she meet Claudia she didn't get the sense that she was a materialistic person so all this that Craig thought, was pure nonsense in his mother's eyes, to her love would prevail but until then all she could do was support him and be there if he needed her.

A couple of semesters had passed and Craig was feeling very confident in himself, more than he ever did, he wanted to pick up the phone and share his enthusiasm with Claudia but couldn't get the courage to do so. As he looked out his bedroom window it started to rain and Craig thought about the first date he had with her and how they played in the rain like two love struck teenagers, how he missed kissing her and caressing her. All he wanted to do was to hold her and tell her how much he loved her and that all this was for her. He kept thinking about how peaceful she looked in the mornings when he awoke before her, and layed there and stared at her with all her natural beauty, he just hoped that there was nobody that had taken his place and maybe just maybe she would wait and be there with open arms, but of course that was his wishful thinking, in all reality that was a long shot for anyone and not even he could possible think of waiting had it been the opposite but hope and faith is what he had to keep him going . . . .

As the day progressed the phone rang, it was Hank, "Hey man how's it going? Haven't heard from you in a long while so I thought I'd pick up the phone and see if you where still breathing or something, I ran into . . . . what's her name . . . oh yeah Claudia and I asked her about you and she ran off like I was diseased or something, she looked really good should of given the broad a chance, hey thought the two of you where dating or something, anyways made me think of you so I called, not like that but you know what I mean, thought some of the guys could get together for some poker." before Hank could finish Craig interrupted, "Hey man she's not a broad and yeah we are together just really busy with our careers," Hank interrupts, "Careers, what careers, I know she's on top but you" Hank laughing, continues, "You work but I wouldn't consider that a career, but whatever just wanted to get a couple of guys together for poker, so you in?" Craig enraged responds, "See dude that's why you had no chance with her or anybody for that matter, last I heard your still alone pushing prostitutes for a good time! Do me a favor leave me and her the F— alone go F— yourself!!!!!!!!" With that said Craig slammed the phone and began to pace up and down the room. Who the hell was he to say crap about him, hadn't heard from the son of a b— in who knows how long and he want's to come out with bull, Craig was so upset that he wanted to punch a hole in someones face. As he continued to pace he heard Claudia's voice in the back of his mind and slowly started to calm down, taking a breath and exhaling . . . . As minutes passed Craig came back to normal and brought his temper down, the only thing now is that every memory Craig has of Claudia was racing in his head and pain grew to much to bare so he headed to a local bar to try to ease the pain . . . .

As Craig walked into Lulu's the memories of Claudia had consumed him, it probably was a bad idea to walk into this bar because that's where they first met, but maybe just maybe she would be there with Lola like old times, and maybe he would be able to explain why he left like he did. But instead of making it better his pain felt worse, as he sat at the bar, he ordered his first scotch and water and swallowed them down as fast as they were coming, before he knew it, he hit rock bottom, and all the pain he was feeling took over his body and reality finally hit him, Claudia was out of his life, how could he have been so stupid! He should of just told her his plans and she would of understood, instead he took off like a coward!!! And now he's having to deal with his lose, the love of his life, he would never feel the same for anyone ever again and at that point it was to much for Craig to handle . . . .

As Craig began to order another drink the bartender cut him off, "That's enough for you buddy, you want me to call you a cab, or a friend, or someone?" Craig responded with a slurred speech, "No slanks, I sink I'll walk," Bartender responds, "No offense buddy, but

I don't think you can handle that either, if you wait I don't mind dropping you off, would hate to see you on the morning news, so do me a favor and wait OK? I'll make you a cup of coffee." Bartender turned around to talk to the other bartender with a whisper, "Keep a eye on him OK? Kinda feel sorry for the guy, think he lost his girlfriend or something he's been talking to himself about her all night, been down that road and a broken heart is no joke, so do that OK?" the 2nd bartender reply's, "No problem boss, try my best." As Craig layed slumped over the bar he pick up his head to clean the sweat from his face when he heard a sweet voice coming from the left side of the bar, "You OK over there?" He glanced over to see a blurred figure of a woman, who at this point looked like Claudia, "Yeah, I will be, you OK over there?" Craig answers back, The woman began to chuckle, and she responds, "That depends on you, if you want company or not." "Be rude of me to say no don't you think?" Craig responds. So the woman grabs her purse and makes her way towards Craig, as she walks over, the bartender hands him his coffee, "Be done in a minute, looks like you have company, so holla when your ready," Craig try's to get a grip of himself. As she begins to sit down, Craig stops her, "Hey been here a long time why don't we head over to your place?" Without hesitation the woman agrees, and the bartender nods his head as a sign that he gets it and that Craig found his way out of the bar and not alone . . . .

When Craig arrived at the woman's apartment everything was a blur, before he knew it, the alcohol and loneliness had taken over his body, and so with that he gave in to lust and for that moment his pain subsided, and as he released the demons from his body, the guilt took over, and as he relieved himself from her, the alcohol faded away and a dark shadow of himself lingered above him, this is not what he wanted to be, and this is not what he was gonna allow himself to become. He pulled his pants up and stared at the woman and apologized, "I'm sorry, this wasn't suppose to happen, I don't know you and you don't know me . . . ." Before he could finish the woman put her finger over his lips and responded, "Shh, you don't have to explain, I know, I felt your pain, and you did me a favor, so walk away with no shame, this was a mutual thing, hope everything works out with you and whoever it is, she is lucky to be so loved." And with that said, Craig left with no intentions to look back, but only forward, he was going to get back the woman he left behind . . . .

Chapter 12

Three years have passed since the success of Claudia's fashion line and it's been a life changing experience for her. With Lola by her side the days have gone by easier and with the frequent trips of her Mom and sisters her longing for family has subsided making her career more pleasant than anticipated. She purchased a house outside of Jersey and doesn't mind the trips back and forth to work and her long trips away because when work slows down she enjoys coming home and relaxing in a place she calls her own and with her family coming down more often, theirs plenty of room for everyone to sleep, so life has been good to her and she is happy that she has what she has.

With the success of her career, life is good, but there still is a place in her heart that hasn't healed and it longs for the man that she will always love. During the past years not once did Craig ever make a attempt to call or get in touch with her, and till this day, she never understood why or what she did, that was so bad, he couldn't leave her an explanation. It still haunts her and makes it difficult to date, so she buries herself in her work once again, to take away the pain and make excuses to why she doesn't bother with a man, besides she already had everything she needed or wanted, no man needed to provide anything for her and being independent made her ecstatic.

It was fall and something Claudia dreaded was around the corner, her birthday. She was hitting the big 43! Not something she was excited about but couldn't avoid. Lola and Tony, her assistant, kept bringing it up so eventually she knew she had to deal with it. After careful thinking Claudia finally decided that she wanted a party, why not, she was successful and had some time off coming so why not celebrate her birthday big. It wasn't the big 40, which she avoided, and it was an odd number, but why not, she deserved it, so party it was. She gave all the details of what she wanted to Tony, he loved putting parties together for her, pink and black and plenty of bling, martini's and Italian cuisine, she wasn't to keen about a club party and preferred it at her house but after Tony explained the mess she would have to clean, the club wasn't a bad idea after all. So with all the details put in place her party was set for Saturday the 19th of November. Everybody that was affiliated with fashion was going to be there. Claudia scheduled a flight for her mom and sisters but since there were no babysitters available for all her nephews and nieces, her mom decided to stay behind with the grand kids, and they brought there husbands along instead, Claudia was excited.

For the party Claudia decided to wear Versace, it was always nice to wear someone else's design besides her own, she wanted sexy for a change, real sexy, something to throw everyone off. Just because she was 43 didn't mean she had to look it, so change was good. As she arrived to her party and exited the car, she wore a beautiful black studded gown with a slit that ran all the way down her leg, showing more than she would on a usual bases. She was a thick girl but not fat, so every curve stood out in a positive way. Let's just say she wore the dress, the dress did not wear her. She was a top plus size fashion designer, so she knew exactly what she could put off! The top dropped low enough to leave to the imagination, elegant, and sexy, Claudia was feeling fabulous!

As she made her way threw the crowd, trying to say hello to everyone possible, low and behold, there standing sophisticated and handsome as ever, she has to admit, was Sammy. The one who gave her a hard time when she was with Craig.

Sammy takes a deep breath and looks right into her eyes, before he speaks, she leans over to give him a hug and Claudia begins to speak first, "Why hello handsome, it's nice of you to join me in celebration of this wonderful day, the birth of ME!" The both of them laugh, Sammy responds, "Haven't changed a bit, still about you, but then again that's the way it should be." Claudia continues, "Want a drink, plenty of martini's any way you desire, but let me see if I remember, hummm . . . . ah yes, dry martini with two olives not one, and a small glass of water with lemon on the side to wash away the after taste, see I still remember." Sammy responds, "Not bad, but minus the water, I've grown up since then." They both continue to laugh. Claudia continues to talk, "Well if you don't mind I'm going to have to excuse myself, I don't want to be a bad hostess at my own party, so I'll leave you to mingle and try not to get into trouble since it's something that you do all to well." Sammy leans over and kisses her on the corner of her lips, and leans over to whisper to her, "Oh the trouble will begin after the party best believe that, so don't disappear on me now I'll be waiting and watching and by the way, you look very sexy in that dress, I can make you feel even sexier and that's a promise." Claudia started to feel the heat rise up from her face as she walked away, Sammy was a dangerous man in every way possible but it's been so long since she's felt a man's touch so maybe Sammy would be the one, only time would tell and the martini's, if that was something she wanted to do, oh what the heck, she thought, she was 43 and grown so Sammy would get lucky tonight and her body would get that needed quench she missed and needed so much.

Everybody was having a wonderful time at Claudia's party, Tony took his wife, Lola had her boyfriend with her, and her sisters and spouses too, all letting loose and having fun as it should be. As Claudia made her way through the crowd to freshen up in the little girls room, as she turned, she didn't know if it was the alcohol or him, but a guy stood at the end of the room who looked just like Craig.

As she got closer, her heart began to beat faster and faster, if it was him, what was she going to say? Or better yet, what was she going to do? Just as she was getting ready to approach him, he turned, it wasn't him. The happiness that Claudia was feeling turned into sadness, deep down she really wanted it to be Craig. As happy as she was, that moment turned it around, and all she wanted to do was go home and call it a night. All the memories that she had with Craig started to fill her head and she wanted to cry. As she headed back to the crowd Lola recognized the change in her attitude. "Hey girl, are you OK?" Claudia responds trying to keep her compulsion, "Yes, why do you ask?" Lola responds surprised, "Why do I ask? You only came back from freshening up looking worse than you did when you left, so yeah I'm asking what is wrong with you?" Claudia takes a breath and continues, "While I was heading to the restroom

I could of sworn that I saw Craig, but don't worry it wasn't, so It kinda ruined my mood." Lola responds very agitated, "Craig, are you serious? I should of known, look girl don't let him get to you on this day, it's your birthday, and you haven't heard from him in about three years, so don't start now, your gonna regret it, besides Sammy's waiting for you, all night I might add, so cheer up and get your party on, OK? OK, get over it!" And with that said Lola walked off and the party continued.

It was 2:00 in the morning and Claudia couldn't wait to kick off her heels and crawl into bed. She was tipsy but not drunk, she wasn't going to embarrass herself by giving the press something to talk about, so she kept it professional even though it was her birthday. Her sisters headed out early back to her house and Lola was going to go get something to eat. Tony and his wife also left early, as he said earlier Sammy was waiting for her and Claudia hoped that he forgotten, but that's what she get's for flirting.

As she walked towards him she didn't want to admit it, but she felt a little excited, it's been awhile since she's felt a man's manhood, so her hormones where racing a bit, but is this what she really wanted? She's was never one for a one night stand or sex just because, it's always had to mean something to her and it's never been the same since Craig but time wasn't slowing down for nobody and Sammy did desire her in the worst way, so why not she thought.

As he drove his car around, Claudia got in, "Where to" Claudia ask, "Anywhere you want to go beautiful" Sammy responds, Claudia continues, "My family is staying at my house, so what about where your at, unless someone has your key," Claudia smirks, "Real funny" Sammy responds and continues "Nobody has the key to my heart but you baby that's why I keep coming back" As Claudia hears him talk she remembers why it didn't last, he was so arrogant and always thought he was all that, if he would lose the attitude maybe he would be, but to her it always made a difference on her opinion of him. Claudia continues to talk, "Enough with the pick up lines, I'm already in the car, just know Sammy that this doesn't mean I'm committed to you, I just need someone to hold me tonight and you happen to be the one, that's all it is." Sammy responds, "Ouch couldn't you have cut me a little deeper, OK, I'll leave it at that for now, but after tonight we will see where you stand." See what I mean, arrogance, she thought. As they drove up to the hotel, Claudia had Craig on her mind, as she did every day that she wasn't working to hard, and even when she did work, she still made time to think of him. She missed him so much but the only one that really knew and understood was her Mom, because Claudia's Mom was the only one that did not judge her for loving someone as much as she loved Craig.

As they approached the room Claudia was racing with emotions, her body wanted to be there, but her mind and heart did not, so she felt confused, does she follow her body and regret it in the morning? Or does she follow her heart and mind and thank herself in the morning? She needed to think fast because the situation was only progressing. As he opened the door a bottle of champagne was waiting for them, for what she didn't know, and really didn't want to know, but it was Sammy so anything was possible.

"Sit down Beautiful and make yourself comfortable." Sammy tells Claudia, "I'm comfortable" Claudia responds. Sammy looks at her with a weird look on his face and confused but continues with his plans with her. As he pops open the bottle he begins to speak, "Here's to us, and I know you said there's no us, but a guy can hope and pray that a girl changes her mind." How ridiculous Claudia thought, and as she smiles shes thinking, if he continues like this sleeping is all I'm going to do, he needs to change his game. As Claudia continues to go with the flow, she makes the toast with him and drinks her champagne. As he takes the glass from her hand, Claudia begins to shake, it has been awhile and she is very nervous. As Sammy picks up this vibe from her, he begins to make it work in his favor.

He begins to kiss her slowly, and if there's one thing that Claudia remembers about Sammy, is that he was a good kisser! He would bring you to your knees. As he has her mesmerized by his kiss, he begins to run his hands down her breast and down her thighs, as he begins foreplay, Claudia's mind wonders away from the kiss and starts thinking about Craig. She no longer is locked by kiss and what started to feel good, started to feel uncomfortable, she just couldn't do it. She was not that kind of woman, and even though she thought her body was craving it, it was not enough to continue, so she stops him. "I CAN'T DO THIS!" Claudia says with a loud voice, Sammy responds alarmed, "Calm down, it's OK, I want to be with you Claudia, but I'm not going to make you do something that you don't want to do! I didn't force you to be here!" Claudia calms down and responds, "I'm sorry Sammy I thought that I could do this but I can't, I didn't mean to put you through this, hope you don't hate me?"

Sammy responds frustrated but understanding how she feels, "I don't hate you Claudia, in my own way I've always loved you and I will have love for you always, there's something about you, your independence, your sexy, your smart, I can go on and on, but my life style and you don't mix, I get it, but just thought I'd try one more time." Claudia sits there quietly then responds, "You know, had you said that earlier instead of that line you pulled, you might have gotten some, but no, you had to pull arrogance," They both laugh, Claudia continues, "If anything Sammy I hope we can remain friends, you do make me laugh." Sammy responds, "Friends? I've never had a woman friend, that's odd, but we can try it, friends it is." Sammy continues, "So can friends cuddle to sleep?" Claudia thinks for a minutes then responds, "I would like that, just cuddle right?" Sammy laughs, "Yes Beautiful, just cuddle." And with that said the both of them fell asleep, Sammy holding Claudia and Claudia feeling safe for the moment . . . .

Chapter 13

With her birthday way behind her, Claudia returns to work with a different aspect on her love life, well actually she doesn't have one, but it was time she did. Even though she was 43 she felt reborn and with her Career being such a success, it was time for her to slow down and start living, besides she wasn't getting any younger and she still had it in her to find someone, besides she did find Craig and he was 23 when she met him so she was excited to try and date again and start a new chapter in her life.

Lately Claudia had been feeling a bit tired more than usual, but with her heavy schedule she thought it was work over load, so she decided to go ahead and get a check up, as she was headed to the doctors office her phone rang, "Hey Claudia it's Tony, had a question on one of the designs for Saturday's fashion show, you need to come see what I'm talking about." Claudia responds, "Let me finish here with the doctor and I'll be right over." See work never ends, Claudia see's the doctor and He decides to run routine test on her, but for now everything seems to be OK, the doctor just advises her to slow down a bit, which she feels she can't, but possibly will have to take the doctor's advice, Claudia hates the fact that all she wants to do is sleep.

As Claudia makes her way back to work, she stops by the Deli to pick up lunch, as she enters the cute little deli shop she notices this tall, not bad looking, husky, well dressed man looking at her, as she makes her way to put in her order, he turns around to talk to her, "Hello, if you don't mind me saying you should try the Hula sandwich, I think you would enjoy it very much, you look like a tropical kind of girl, if you don't mind me saying." Claudia responds with a smile, "As a matter of fact I was thinking of ordering that, there's something about bean sprouts in a sandwich, it enhances the flavor for some strange reason." Enhances the flavor, as Claudia thought about that statement she wanted to die! How stupid was that? Can't blame him if he doesn't respond she thought. While she continued with her business he continues to talk, "Sorry to be so rude, my name is David, David Williams, and you are?" Claudia extends her hand, "Well hello David my name is Claudia, Claudia Cruze." Mr. Williams continues, "I usually don't make it a habit to go around suggesting food items off the menu, but being that I did, and if you don't have any plans tonight I was wondering if maybe you wanted to go to dinner with me and possibly discuss bean sprouts and it's wonders on your taste buds?" Claudia can feel the heat rise up her face and she begins to blush, but with a smile responds, "Funny, but you know, I don't make it a habit excepting invitations from people who hang around deli's giving menu advice either." Both of them begin to laugh, Claudia continues, "But it would be nice to talk sprouts over dinner and since I really don't have anything planned, dinner sounds nice." Mr. Williams responds, "Well great how about 8:00 at Manicotti's?" Before he could finish Claudia interrupts, "I'm not sure about Manicotti's but I heard of a real nice seafood restaurant down from there if you don't mind? This is really odd, what if your a serial killer, or rapist?" Mr. Williams laughs, "Little to late now don't you think? I admit this is fast pace, but for some reason I feel comfortable talking to you so I guess it's a safe sign for both of us." Claudia responds, "Yes I understand what your saying, it does feel comfortable, so dinner it is, I'll met you at 8:00, seafood restaurant, right?" Mr. Williams responds with excitement in his voice, "Seafood it is." So with that said Claudia grabbed her lunch, waved goodbye and headed back to work, for the first time, in a long time, she was excited.

The work day seemed very long for a short day, Tony, her assistant had her going in circles which really wasn't out of the ordinary for Claudia, it was the usual hustle and bustle in the office. Claudia was planning a business trip to Russia and was very excited. Her fall fashion line was a big success and talk of her fashion show was causing a bit of a media frenzy, there were so many of the little things to take care of before she went. It was 6:00 and Claudia's body was feeling drained, as she sat there in her office she began to doze off, as her mind started to drift she visioned herself walking in a field of bean sprouts and that's when she jumped up and awoke startled, she had a date!

As she scurried through the office, looking for her things, she heard a knock at the door. "What now?" Claudia yelled, "I don't have time for anymore questions, Tony if it's you can this wait for tomorrow?" There was a long silence, Claudia continued, "Tony?"

Frustrated and tired, Claudia walked to the door ready to give Tony an ear full when to her surprise its Craig.

Craig stood there, at the door with flowers in his hand, he had on a suit and looked like he had put on some weight, but in a good way, it looked good on him. Claudia stood there with a blank look on her face, frozen, motionless, as if someone walked in from the dead, she didn't know if she wanted to hit him and hurt him or hug him, at that moment she didn't know what to feel.

"Hello Claudia, these are for you, I was hoping to catch you in your office, may I sit down?" You could hear the nervousness in Craig's voice, Claudia stood there speechless, after she silently put herself together she responded, "I see no reason for you to sit down and make yourself comfortable, I really don't have time to hear what you have to say, I have a date in a hour and I don't want to keep him waiting, oh but that's something you know all to well, keeping someone waiting." Before she could continue Craig interrupts, "Look Claudia I don't even know where to begin with all this, or how to even try to validate things but could you please just sit down and try to hear me out?" Claudia tries to keep her composure but responds with a elevated voice, "Hear you out?! What could you possible say to me that's gonna make up for THREE YEARS, THREE YEARS CRAIG? I went through many emotions trying to figure it out! You want me to give you time? Well I don't have time, so please find your way out, and don't bother trying to get a hold of me, I don't want to hear what you have to say!" As Claudia spoke to Craig he sat there and starred at her with sadness in his eyes but took whatever it was she had to say, after she finished, he spoke, "I made the mistake of walking away the first time, I guarantee you that I will not make that same mistake twice, I'm going to go for now, but listen to me, no matter what it takes I will get you to sit and listen, maybe not today, or tomorrow, or the next couple of months for that matter, but it will happen, so I'm going to leave you with this, I love you Claudia, I've never stopped loving you, because of you I am what I am today. As much as I regret saying this enjoy your night." As he began to walk away he stopped, kissed her on her check, and whispered, "I never stopped loving you . . . ."

As Craig walked out of the office Claudia slammed the door behind him! As she stood there in disbelief it hit her, Craig was back! As reality started to sink in, her tears began to fill her eyes and she sat there and cried, uncontrollably, like a little girl with so much sentiment, it was an emotion she couldn't stop.

After what seemed like a lifetime, Claudia finally started pulling herself together, she had a date in 15 minutes and she wasn't going to cheat herself, so she needed to get it together, as for the moment her life had been turned upside down but Claudia knew that for the next couple of hours she wasn't going to allow herself to fall apart, she would get through this . . . .

Running about 20 minutes late, Claudia finally made her way into the restaurant, David was sitting there waiting patiently at the bar. As she sat down they said there hellos and right away David asked her, "I don't know anything about you but if you don't mind me asking what's wrong? You look so different than you did this afternoon, if you need some time we could schedule dinner another day?" As David talked tears ran down Claudia's face, as she held back her tears she began to explain, "I really want to stay and have dinner with you and get to know you, you seem like a very nice person, but if I do it wouldn't be fair to you. Right before I got here someone who left my life came back into my life, it's left me angry, confused, and who knows what else. My stomach is in knots and all I really want to do is go home." David responds, "Look Claudia, I would like to say that I understand but I don't, so whenever your ready, give me a call, and if I have time I'll join you." With that said David walked away. At that point Claudia could care less, so she grabbed her purse and headed back home.

When she arrived home the first thing she did was call her assistant Tony, it was 11:00pm when she made the call. Tony with a sleepy voice, answers, "Hello, Ms. Claudia, are you OK, did I miss a order, or appointment?" Claudia responds, "No, no Tony, I'm sorry to wake you, I just wanted you to know that I'm not feeling well so could you handle all my appointments tomorrow, I really would appreciate it?" Tony, now fully awake, responds, "Are you OK? You never miss work, even sick, do you need me to send someone over?" Claudia continues, "No I just need a day or two, just do me a favor and call me only if necessary, I know you can handle things." Confused, Tony responds, "You got it Ms. Claudia, you know I can, hope you feel better." So with everything set for tomorrow Claudia falls asleep . . . .

The morning came and went and Claudia still layed there in bed, with so many thoughts running through her mind she couldn't get the energy to get out of bed. How could Craig possible think, that after all these years, it would be OK to come back, and try to explain what she needed to know a long time ago. What would she be showing him if she allowed him to explain? She wasn't some weak young naive girl, nor was she going to allow him to manipulate his way back to her! Then she thought what if he doesn't want to come back? What if he left her for another woman and couldn't get the courage to tell her? All these thoughts where driving her crazy!

Maybe she needed to talk to him and let him explain, for piece of mind on her part, it seemed like she was the only person loosing her mind lately.

It was 5:00 o'clock in the afternoon and Claudia finally made her way out of bed, as she walked to the kitchen to make herself something to eat, the door bell rang, what now Claudia thought. As she looked out the peep hole she couldn't really tell who was there, so she slowly opened the door, it was Lola. Lola looked at Claudia surprised, she had never seen Claudia in the condition she was in, "OK what is going on?" Lola ask Claudia, Claudia responds trying to keep herself together, "Nothing, I just don't feel good that's all." Lola continues, "Bull! I've known you longer than that, it's not a under the weather look for you, I'm going to ask you again so be honest because I'm not leaving till I get the answer that I'm happy with." Claudia walks to the kitchen and Lola follows, then Claudia begins to speak, "Yesterday when I was getting ready to leave the office for my date, Craig showed up, he wanted to explain himself Lola but as much as I wanted to hear it I threw him out, I don't know if I want to hear what he has to say anymore, I don't know if it even matters." Before Claudia could continue Lola responds, "Wow, he finally gathered up enough nerve to come and face you, I want to say so many things about him right now Claudia but because your my girl, I'm not, if you didn't care about what he had to say you wouldn't be home right now looking like hell, you'd be at work getting ready for your big trip, so I will refrain from saying what I truly think about him." Claudia responds, "You know Lola I know you've never liked Craig even though you've never said anything, I don't know if it's the age difference or what but things where going really good between us that's why it's so hard to understand why he left like he did." Lola interrupts, "I never disliked him, I always thought you could do better, here you are top fashion designer and you can have anything you want! Any man, anything, you make your own happiness and instead you settled for a boy, a boy, someone with nothing to offer you but heartache," before Lola could finish Claudia begins to talk, "Wait a minute!, Craig is not a boy! He's 28! and last I heard that was considered a man! How dare you, you didn't even know what our relationship entailed, what we talked about, our dreams together, he never liked the fact that I made as much money as I did, he wanted better, so who are you to judge?! I loved him! And you know what? I still do, and what makes you think that a older man is going to treat me better or not want anything from me? Men are men at any age, so how can you judge someone by that?" After Caudia finished talking she stormed out of the kitchen, into her room and slammed the door! As Lola sat there she thought about what she said and she thought about what Claudia said and she began to feel bad. She still didn't agree with Claudia but maybe she was being a bit hard on Craig, she really didn't know him as well as she wanted to, and maybe she was a bit jealous because he took Claudia's time from her, whatever the reason Claudia was her friend and she needed to make things right. So Lola decided that from here on she was going to listen and if Claudia needed her to put in her two cents, she would, if not she would just be the shoulder to cry on.

Lola made her way to Claudia's room, right before Lola begins to knock, Claudia calls out, "You can come in." Lola looks at Claudia and begins to speak, "You mad at me?" Claudia responds, "No, I'm not mad, I just have all this anger and I don't know how to handle it." Lola continues, "Well it looks to me that deep down you want to talk to Craig, so maybe you should, but in your terms. I think you owe it to yourself to find out what happened, it's gonna tear you apart girl if you don't, besides you said it yourself, you still love him." Claudia began to think, did she say that? Maybe it was the heat of the moment, then her heart began to ache, she still was in love with him and talking to him was going to be what she needed to mend her heart and move on with her life. As the both of them sat there they gave each other a hug, Claudia turns and tells Lola, "What would I do without you friend?" Lola responds, "The same thing I would do without you, be lost, so with that said get up and shower because the funk is getting ready to take over you girl, not having it." Both of them begin to laugh and Claudia, feeling much better, jumps into the shower . . . .

Chapter 14

Claudia was ready for her trip to Russia, it was going to be one of the biggest events in her career! Claudia decided to take her whole office staff on this trip, it was something she felt they all deserved, everyone was excited. Tony was getting the last minute details together, Lola was getting the models together and Claudia was trying to get herself together. Even though it was a trip that everyone was ecstatic about, Claudia also reminded them that it was a business trip as well, in a country that was very different and rules had to be followed precisely, everyone needed to be on top of everything, so to keep everyone's mind right Claudia send everyone home early, she felt they could get a good nights rest and be focused, everyone needed to be on a professional level.

As she gathered her things for the day, the phone rang, there wasn't anyone in the office so she decided to let the answering machine pick it up, she was glad she did because it was Craig,

"Claudia? I was hoping to catch you in your office but I guess your getting ready for your big trip, saw a small article in the paper about it, just wanted to wish you a safe journey, and if you would like to call me when you get back, I'll be here." Claudia stood there staring at the phone, deep down she really wanted to pick it up and talk to him but for the moment it was best if she didn't, the timing was all wrong, it would have to be when she was ready and on her terms, right now all she needed to do was worry about her trip and nothing else, so Craig would have to wait.

It was 5:00 in the morning when Claudia's alarm went off, she felt like she hadn't slept in days, the doctor had prescribed medicine to give her an extra boost but it didn't seem to help, all she wanted to do was stay in bed. She ached from head to toe and it was beginning to take a toll on her, but she couldn't let it stop her so she forced herself out of bed and into the shower it was something that became more frequent with her but something she adjusted to. Tony scheduled a limo to pick up everyone and Claudia asked to be picked up last, as she made her way to the car, everyone began to clap, Claudia responded with a laugh, "Really guys, it's not that big a deal, just enjoy, but at the same time be responsible because all of you are representing me." With that said, Tony responds, "Um mm no Ms. Claudia, I think everyone clapped because we've been in your driveway for 20 min. and we never thought you would make it out in time to catch our plane." Everybody hesitated and looked at Claudia waiting for a response, before anyone could say anything Claudia began to laugh uncontrollably, and without anything else being said, they made there way to the airport.

As they arrived in Russia they where surprised with the welcoming they received, it was a bit overwhelming for Claudia, but well worth it, her clothing line is a big success and she couldn't feel anymore proud, she was on top of the world. Everything worked out as planned, Tony, her assistant always went beyond what his job entailed and Claudia was very blessed to have him. As they wrapped up the show Claudia asked Tony to make reservations for everyone at one of there famous restaurants in Moscow, Claudia was feeling successful as ever. As everyone sat there at the dinner table Claudia stood up and made a toast, "I would like to thank everyone for there hard work and participation in making this show a success, I'm so blessed to have people like you guys working for me, you are like family and I thank you." As she sat down tears filled her eyes, just then Lola stood up to speak, "Claudia, it's been awhile since the first time we met, you were that enthusiastic woman eager to make her mark in this business, you came in and took control, you made a name for plus size women all over the world, you broke barriers, but more important than that, you took me in and made me family, you are like a sister that I never had, and I thank you, for remembering me in your journey and bringing me along to work with you, it has been a blessing." Before you knew it there wasn't one dry eye at the table, just then Tony began to speak, "OK, that's enough on the mush, with Ms. Claudia's permission I have something to say." Claudia nodded her head with a yes gesture, knowing exactly what he was going to say, "When we get back to work, there are going to be changes, Ms. Claudia will be opening up a boutique in Manhattan, she's been working on it for several months now and it's almost ready, so some of our office management will be moved around with great incentives, the unveiling of the boutique is in 1 month and we are very excited. The name of the boutique is a secret till the opening, so expect busy schedules, and plenty of readjustments." Everyone at the table began to clap, Claudia responds, "OK everyone I hope you know that this is positive change, nobody will be making less than what they make now just because of the changes, who ever works over there is just as important to me as if you worked with me now, some of you will be getting a raise, so this is definitely a good thing, so no worries my friends, no worries." With all that said they enjoyed there dinner, laughing and mingling the rest of the night. As Claudia sat back she looked on with so much happiness, this is exactly where she wanted to be.

The trip back was definitely exhausting for everyone, as always Claudia had a difficult time getting up in the morning, so she was a bit cranky but only because she didn't feel good, she was taking the medicine the doctor had prescribed but it really wasn't helping her, she made up her mind that when she returned she needed to make a visit back to the doctor, the way her body felt made her dread her plane ride home, it was going to be a long one.

Finally Claudia and her staff hit U.S. soil, she was so happy to be back home. She said her goodbyes to everyone and headed to her home, as she made it to the front door she couldn't wait to open it, everything was nice and quiet the way she like it. As she made herself comfortable, she lay ed on the sofa and started to watch a movie, for some reason her mind started to drift and Craig popped into her mind. It had been awhile since she thought of him, probably because she was to busy to stop and think of anything or anyone else. But it was nice, she began to think of how things where before he left, then she wondered if maybe it was time to hear what he had to say, curiosity was taking a toll on her, and she deserved an explanation. It was hard for her because she didn't know if she really wanted to bring back all those feelings she locked away deep in her heart. And then it scared her a little, what if the love was gone? If anything, she wanted to hold on to what ever was left, so it was difficult for her to hear Craig out. As her mind continued to go 100 miles an hour she fell asleep.

Claudia had given everyone Monday off, even Tony, so she wasn't in a hurry to get up and go to work, she figured she would make her way in about noon. She had a few clients to get a hold of and some boutique business, but it was nothing she couldn't handle alone. As she made her way out of bed she noticed that her feet and legs had such an excruciating pain, she could feel bolts of pain shooting through her calves, for a moment she started to panic. As she made her way back to the bed she decided to call Lola, she couldn't go through this alone anymore. The phone rang three times before Lola answered, "Hey Claudia, how's it going? Do you want to meet for breakfast?" Before Claudia could respond she began to cry." Lola responds worried, "WHAT'S WRONG, ANSWER ME GIRL?!" Claudia speaks, "I'm sorry Lola I didn't mean to scare you but I really don't feel well and I was wondering if you could take me down to the emergency room?" Before she could finish Lola responds, "I'M ON MY WAY!" Within 20 minutes Lola was there.

When Lola got there she was shocked! A few days ago Claudia was busy, moving, working, but today she couldn't even get out of bed, Lola began to panic. In a faint voice Claudia tells her to call an ambulance, the pain had worsened so much that she couldn't even move. Lola made the call and before to long the ambulance arrived.

They made there way to the hospital and Claudia barely had any strength to talk, the pain was so overwhelming that it took all she had. Lola was in complete shock, she had no idea that Claudia was even sick, she had to get herself together for her friend, Claudia needed her now more than ever. As the hospital admitted Claudia, Lola needed to make some decisions, the first person she called was Claudia's assistant, Tony, he needed to keep everything in line at work, next she needed to call her mother, Lola hesitated a bit, she wanted to get all the facts before she worried her, she didn't wanted to sound like an idiot, so she decided that when she got information she would call. As time went by the nurse finally let Lola come in to be with Claudia, she looked a little bit better after the doctors gave her medicine for the pain. As Lola sat quietly beside her Claudia began to speak, "I'm so sorry Lola, I didn't want to scare you but I didn't know who to call," Lola interrupted, "Don't even go there, I'm glad I could be here with you, why didn't you tell me you weren't feeling good and what exactly is wrong with you?" Claudia responds, "They really don't know, I have a virus but they don't know how, or where it started, so from time to time I get these weak spells, so there trying to get it where it's controlled until they can figure it out." "Is it AIDS?" Lola ask carefully, "No Lola it's not AIDS, once they get it under control I'll be OK, I just need to rest, that's all." Lola laughs, "I know I can say stupid things at times," Waiting for a response Lola notices that Claudia's asleep, so she sits on the chair next to her and dozes off.

Lola had lost track of time, she had been at the hospital all day with Claudia, she got up to stretch a bit and walk around the hospital when Claudia's nurse walked in, Lola decided to ask questions, "I'm like sister to her and I was wondering if I could ask you some questions?" The nurse responds, "Are you Lola, because if you are she has you down as next of kin in cause of an emergency, so you can ask all the questions, you want." Lola's eyes began to water and she responded, "Next of kin? Is she going to die? I just want to know if she's going to be OK." The nurse responds, "Oh no sweetie, she's not going to die, she's going to be OK, we just have to find that stubborn virus infection she has and once we get it under control she's gonna be fine." After the nurse finished explaining she could see that Lola was overwhelmed so she hugged her and reassured her that everything was going to be OK. The nurse continued, "She probably will get to go home tomorrow so why don't you go home and get some rest." Lola, holding back her tears, agrees. As she was gathering her things Claudia wakes up, "Are you leaving?" Lola responds, "Yes girl, gonna go get some rest since you might be getting out tomorrow, I'll be her first thing in the morning OK?" Claudia responds, "OK, hey you haven't called my mother have you? If you haven't I would appreciate it if you don't, there's no need in worrying her if I'm going home tomorrow, so do me the favor and don't call her." Lola responds, "I haven't called her, so whatever you want my friend, I'll leave that up to you." Lola leaned over and gave Claudia a big hug, then she whispers, "Don't ever scare me like that again, you are my only friend in the world, what would I do without you? I'm here to help you get better OK, your not alone, get some rest." And with that Lola left the hospital.

It was the next morning and Lola kept her word, she was there promptly at 7:00, with coffee in her hand she headed up stairs to see Claudia. As she walked in the room Tony was sitting talking with her. Lola being defensive asked, "What do you think your doing? She needs absolute rest Tony, I think the business will be OK for a couple of days, can't you handle things by yourself?!" Tony, upset, responds, "I know that Lola, but there's certain things that are out of my control, like your paycheck, so I needed her signature, or there's no pay!" Lola flustered, responds, "I don't care just make it quick, she need's all the rest she can get, pay or no pay, she needs to get better!" Claudia jumps into the conversation, "OK you two, If you haven't noticed, I'm still here, I appreciate you looking out Lola, that's why I luv ya, but business still needs to go on and that's why I have Tony, so both of you need to relax and let me manage things the way I know how, I'm going to be just fine, so unless you want me to have a heart attack I need the both of you to be civil and behave your-self's, is that to much to ask for?" Both of them shook there shoulders, made a grunt and agreed.

Tony gives Claudia a hug and tells her to get well, before he leaves he turns and gives Lola one of those looks to kill. Claudia laughs and begins to speak to Lola, "You two are a riot, I tell you never a boring moment. The doctor will be in at 9:00 this morning and hopefully he releases me, if he does, will you please stay the night, just in case I have another episode?" Lola responds, "Of course I will, hey we can rent that movie I've been wanting to see with that actress Meg Ryan and Tom Hanks, it's an old one about Email, but still a good one I hear." Claudia shook her head and responds, "I think it's called You Got Mail or something like that, I've seen it but it's been awhile, wouldn't mind seeing it again." With that said Lola excused herself to go get something to drink.

As Claudia waited for the doctor there was a knock at the door, and to her surprise, it was Craig. As he stood there Claudia's heart began to pound, she was so happy that he was there but didn't want him to see her excitement, before she could speak, he begins, "I know I'm probably the last person you wanted to see right now, but when I showed up at your office Tony told me what happened and I needed to see you." Claudia responds, "Tony told you? What happened to confidentiality? Look Craig . . ." Before she could finished Craig interrupts, "Look don't be upset with your assistant, I put him in a very awkward position and he did what he felt was right, I love you Claudia and I know you have a tough time believing me, I don't blame you, I probably would feel the same but fact of the matter is I love you, so I think it's time we have our talk, when your ready but it needs to be done, or I will continue to bother you till I get some time." Claudia lays back in her bed and begins to speak when her doctor walks in, "Look Craig your right, it is time, let me get released from here and I'll call you, this is to much to discuss right here and now." Craig leaned over and whispered in her ear, "That's I'll I'm asking, I love you Claudia." and with that said Craiged walked out.

Before to long Lola made her way back to the room and the doctor was giving Claudia her release papers, "Are you a relative?" the doctor ask Lola, she responds, "Yes I am." The doctor continues, "Make sure she has plenty of rest, I know she has to work but make sure she takes it easy." Lola responds, "Yes sir, your talking to the right person, I will make sure she has plenty of rest." Claudia rolls her eyes and just listens, overwhelmed and ready to go home . . . .

Chapter 15

Claudia was so happy to be home, it was only one day in the hospital but it felt like a eternity to her. After all the poking and test that they where doing she really didn't eat right so she was hungry. Lola helped her get settled in and the both of them decided to order in Chinese, as they sat on Claudia's sofa Lola noticed that she looked lost in thought, "Are you OK?" Lola asked Claudia, Claudia responds, "Before the doctor released me Craig was there to see me" Lola interrupts, "Craig? I hope you told him where to go." Claudia continues, "No, I didn't, I actually want to talk to him Lola, I think I deserve some kind of explanation to why he took off like he did, I'm still in love with him. Now don't get me wrong, I definitely am not letting my guard down, but I want to talk to him, I've been thinking about it and it's time, so I'm calling him tonight." Both of them sat there quiet for a long time, speechless, then Claudia broke the silence, "You think I'm being gullible don't you? You think I'm setting my self up for heartache again. Look Lola I need closure." Lola took awhile before she responded, "I don't think your gullible, I just don't want to see you hurt but at the same time I do understand, I want to hear what he has to say too. You know Claudia at one point I did like the guy and when you two where together I saw how happy you two where, so I've wondered why things turned out the way they did. You'll never know if it's meant to be if you keep avoiding the situation, so give him a call and invite him over, I'll go home and if you need me just call, I'm a phone call away." Claudia jumped up with excitement just like a little girl, she sighs then responds, "Lola you don't know how much I needed you to say that, it's weird but it's like I was waiting for your blessing or something, I don't know I'm just happy you understand." So with all that said Claudia picked up the phone and called Craig, it was finally time for closure and at this moment it didn't matter what the out come would be, she just needed to know why.

Lola and Claudia still had dinner but as soon as they where done Lola left. With her finally gone, Claudia could gather her composure and thoughts, she was so nervous that she began to sweat and her heart began to race, the time was finally here. She paced back and forth when the door bell finally rang, it will be faith that brings them back together or closure to a romance that she will always treasure and be blessed for having . . . .

Craig stood there nervous but anxious to see her, his heart was pounding not knowing what to expect but ready for whatever he was about to deal with. Claudia looked as beautiful as ever, his eyes still glistened when he saw her and loving her was something he never stop doing. Before he could speak Claudia invited him in, "Wow, you have a beautiful home, of course I never expected anything less of you, you have definitely made a name for yourself with Cruse Designs, but then again we all knew that." Claudia smiled and invited him to sit down, "Would you like anything to drink," she asked him, he responds, "I could use a scotch and water." Claudia responds, "Wow, big time huh, I remember when you didn't know what a cosmo was, now your hitting it like the big boys." Craig continues, "I still don't drink Claudia, but I think I could use one right now, to loosen my nerves." Claudia smirks, "I'm sorry I didn't mean anything bad by it, of course scotch and water coming up." There was silence before Claudia begins to speak, "So how have you been? You look good Craig, it looks like you've put on some weight." Craig responds, "Yes I've put on some pounds here and there, I was tired and depressed so I started hitting the gym, I go about three times a day, you look wonderful Claudia, and you haven't changed, still glamorous as ever." Claudia smiles and responds, "OK Craig, let's stop the small talk and get down to why your here, I'm going to be blunt, which I think is very appropriate for this time, why did you leave me without any explanation, why? Do you know what that did to me inside? I buried myself in my work so I wouldn't get lost in my pain, everyday I tried to make excuses for you till I realized there was none. If I would of allowed you to you would of destroyed me, but let me tell you something, you didn't, I'm here and stronger than ever, head of my own empire! I loved you and I wanted to share my life with you, but obviously we both where on different pages, different directions in our lives, I just figured you for a survivor but obviously I was wrong you are nothing but a coward and I'm sorry but you made me feel that! NO let me take that back I'm not sorry YOU ARE A COWARD! And right now I'm not sure if there's anything you can say to make things better." Claudia could feel the heat in her face and the blood rush through her veins, when she finished Craig took a deep breath and began to talk, "Your right there's nothing I can say to change things, I was a coward Claudia, but let me tell you why. When I met you you where this talented woman, that amazed me. With every word that came out of your mouth, your style, your personality, everything about you was perfect to me and here I am this young man with only a vision of what I wanted to be, stuck in the same old routine everyday with no way out. Do you think I liked the fact that I couldn't provide for you the way that you where use to? You are a very successful business woman, you didn't need me. I wasn't going to be with you and use your money, I couldn't do that. I do like the simpler things in life, but I also wanted what you had, but I couldn't be part of it if I couldn't contribute." Claudia interrupts, "So you thought that by walking away it was going to make matters better? How could you possibly think that it was OK?" Craig continues, "I didn't plan for things to happen the way they did, when you told me about your big career change I panicked. I was so happy for you but at the same time I was embarrassed about myself. All I could think of was what were you going to tell your coworkers about me? I couldn't carry a conversation about anything and I didn't want to embarrass you, I was embarrassed of myself Do you think I was proud of myself for walking away? I love you Claudia and knowing that I might lose you killed me! It was hard on me too. There where days that I just didn't know if I was coming or going, you were in my heart and mind everyday." Claudia interrupted, "It still doesn't justify walking away, as a matter of fact it angers me knowing that you couldn't trust me enough to tell me how you where feeling, I could of helped you Craig," Craig interrupts, "See that's what I'm talking about, I didn't want your help! Being the caring person you are, you would of want to put me through school, pay my way for me and I just wasn't going to let it happen! I needed to do things on my own, and I did! Granted I should of told you but I was to embarrassed, please understand that it had nothing to do with me not loving you, it's because of how much I do love you that I had to go find myself. Claudia in my eyes I needed to make myself a better person, to give you everything that you deserve and more. I knew I was taking a chance, that maybe when I came back you would be happy with someone else, I knew that, but I prayed and went on FAITH, I knew deep in my heart we where meant for each other and it would work out. I know it's been 3 years since we've seen each other or talked but I'm here and by the looks of it your still single, that means something." Claudia sat there silent for what seemed like forever, as tears flowed down her face she began to talk in a calm low voice, "Craig, even though I have a successful career I still struggled, I struggled with the fact that you walked away leaving me to believe that I didn't mean anything to you. I tried to move on but I couldn't, I was accepting the fact that maybe I was going to be alone for the rest of my life, then here you come wanting me to understand that you did it all for me, how do you expect me to believe that? The fact remains that you didn't believe in me enough to know that I would of done anything you wanted to help you, even leave you alone so you could get it together and find yourself, but you didn't even give me a chance to show you, so how do you expect me to feel? I do know, that sitting here with you right now, my love for you never died, I love you so much, but how can I be sure that every time my career blossoms you get defensive, I'm a FASHION DESIGNER, not some small town seamstress with dreams, my dreams are being fulfilled now, I need someone by my side all the time and not be threatened by my success." Craig sat there lost, this is not how he intended things to be, he always thought that Claudia would be here with open arms but then again why should she, he was a coward, and possibly because of his actions three years ago, he lost Claudia. As Craig began to speak you could here the crack in his voice, he tried very hard not to break down but he was feeling perhaps the way Claudia did when he left, "Oh Baby, there's nothing I can say that will change things, I was wrong and I will apologize for it the rest of my life if I had to, but at the time I thought it was what I needed to do, I'm a business man now and I'm making my 6 digit a year salary and because of you I'm doing it, all I ask is to find it in your heart to forgive me. I am that man that will be by your side no matter what, I will never leave again, I promise you, I came back for you and nobody else, can't you see Claudia, there is nobody else, there never was when we were apart and nobody will ever take your place in my eyes." Tears filled Claudia's eyes and she began to cry uncontrollably, before Craig could speak, he grabbed her and hugged her and he began to cry also, "I'm so sorry Love, I'm so sorry." Both of them held each other for a long time and let out all of the emotions that they both carried for 3 years, it was a good feeling for both, as they put themselves together Craig asked Claudia what he had been anticipating to ask and possibly change there lives, "So where do we go from here?" As he said those words his heart began to race because he had no idea what Claudia's response was going to be. As he sat there she got up and excused herself, the anticipation made Craig's stomach upset, but he waited patiently hoping that things would finally be mended.

Claudia made her way to the kitchen to get a drink, now she needed something to calm her nerves so she poured a glass of wine, as she sat at the bar stool of her kitchen island all kinds of thoughts and emotions were running through her mind. One thing that she was sure of, is the anxiety that she felt all these years, was finally lifted, she had a sense of serenity knowing that Craig still loved her and she wasn't the reason for his actions. But now she needed to decide if she was going to allow Craig back into her life, she was still hurt by the fact that he didn't trust her enough to let her in. As that thought raced through her mind she also evaluated the fact that from a man's point of view he was in a tough spot. Craig was right, she probably would of wanted to pay his way through school, most men would of jumped at the chance for that kind of situation but Craig didn't. She just wished that he would of talked to here and avoided all the pain that was endured, she still loved him as much as the first time she met him and he did come back, so Claudia was confused with her heart and her mind, does she let him in one more time and try for a chance of happiness or does she let him go with a sense of relieve knowing the truth but letting him live with his choices?

As Claudia sat there thinking Craig makes his way to the kitchen, "Need company?" he asked her, "You want a glass of wine?" She responds, "Sure, but not to much, wine doesn't sit well with me." Claudia pours him a glass of wine and continues to speak, "Look Craig I don't know if this is the right thing for me to do in my life, but I'm tired of going through it alone. I do love you, very much, and I've never stopped loving you, I just don't want to get hurt, I'm to old for these high school games, I need to know that you will be here for me when I need you, I need you to hold me when my days gone chaotic, and when I'm gone on business I need someone to greet me when I get home, is that to much to ask?" Craig anxiously answers, "Love I'm going to be that man, I'll be by your side with your career, your everyday routine, I'll be here waiting, I love you, your it for me!" Claudia took a deep breath and let out a sigh of relieve, then she responds with a smile, "I hope we both know what were doing, cause this is it, no more free passes for you OK? It's do or die, metaphorically speaking of course, your stuck with me again, and this time can you get it right please?" Both Craig and Claudia began to laugh, and Craig hugged Claudia so tight she though she was going to pass out. There was a sense of peace that filled the room, and if anyone was there they could feel the love that surrounded them both, it was a feeling that was worth waiting for . . . .

As the night passed both of them felt exhausted, after so many years apart, indulgence in each other would have been the next step, but instead they lay-ed next to each other, holding on, afraid to let each other go, falling into a deep sleep, a peaceful sleep that both of them hadn't had in years.

As the sun came up, there was a knock at the door, Claudia woke up startled and accidentally pushed Craig off the sofa. As they both tried to get themselves together the doorbell rang uncontrollably, Craig annoyed, speaks, "Who the hell is ringing the doorbell like that?!" Claudia, annoyed herself, responds, "If I can make my way over there, I'll find out." Breathing heavy Claudia takes a peek through the peep hole, then responds, "Oh, it's Lola, I forgot to call her." As she opened the door she pushes Lola out closing the door behind her. Lola starts to speak bothered at the fact that she won't let her in, "What's going on! I've been calling you all morning to check on you, you didn't answer so I got worried and rushed over here, then you won't let me in, that's how you show appreciation?" Claudia responds, "Calm down! I'm going to let you in, I just had to brief you right quick, first don't get upset but Craig's in there, and we . . . ." Lola interrupts, "Don't tell me you fell for his bull crap again?" Claudia continues, "It's not bull crap, we are working on it but we are together again, just be happy for me please, I'll give you all the details later, and one more thing, please don't tell him about my episode the other night, I'm not ready to tell him anything about what's going on with my health, can you please promise me that?" Lola grunts and gives her a look, Claudia responds, "Hello? Did you hear me? Don't tell him Lola I'm serious and be nice!" Lola responds, "All right, all right! You are glowing, which is something I haven't seen in a long time, I don't agree with you on not telling him Claudia, I hope you do plan to tell him soon, I thought you didn't like secrets? But I'll keep my mouth shut, and I'll try to be nice, to a certain point." Claudia responds with a smile, "Fine, I appreciate it, OK, now you can come in." As they walked through the foyer Craig was making his way out, "I'm sorry Love I have to go, I have a business meeting at 11:00 this morning but I'm going to call you after so we can get together, I love you." Claudia gives Craig a kiss and responds, "I love you too." As he walked out he turned to greet Lola, with a sarcastic look on her face she smiles at him and walks the opposite way.

As both of them sat down in Claudia's kitchen she began to tell Lola everything that happened that night, she explained why he left and his reasoning's behind it, when she was done Lola sat there a long time with nothing to say. Claudia didn't know if Lola heard her or tuned her out, but after a long while Lola responded, "You know, all these years I thought Craig was a horrible person for what he did to you, I hated him with a passion, and that's a lot of passion coming from me, I couldn't understand how or why he would hurt you. And now you've just explained why, and I don't hate him anymore.

I kind of respect him for not sticking around, if that makes any sense. Sounds like you've finally got your prince charming after all to fit in your castle." Claudia's eyes began to tear as she sits back and embraces Lola's words, she thinks about Lola's statement and smiles, maybe Lola was right, her prince had finally arrived . . . .

Chapter 16

Couple of days had passed and Claudia was back at work, she was afraid to come back to a mess, but like always Tony had it under control. It was 1 week till her big opening of her boutique and she was feeling the pressure. Craig stopped in that morning to check on her, everyone in the office was buzzing about there reunion, Claudia didn't care she carried on her morning without a care in the world. The medicine the doctor prescribed seem to be working, Claudia was full of energy and ready to tackle on her day, for once it was a good time in Claudia's life, everything seemed to be complete.

The days came and went sooner than Claudia could count it was the night before her big opening of the boutique and she was excited. There were many boutiques in New York but what made this one special was it's plus sizes. It was very hard for women of size to find stylish clothes so Claudia was proud to accompany them, big is beautiful and she would just add the touches to make them feel glamorous.

Craig made his way over to Claudia's that night, he had something special planned before her big opening and he couldn't wait to share it with her. As he made his way to the door Claudia was already there opening it for him, she greeted him with a hug and a kiss, "Mm you smell good and look so handsome," She tells him with such happiness, "Why thank you Love and you look so cute with that ponytail on top of your head looking relaxed." Claudia blushed, "I know not one of my better moments." Craig responds, "Are you kidding? I think those are your best! I love seeing you natural and relaxed, I love it!" As they made there way into the house Claudia noticed Craig's enormous smile, she knew he was up to something. "Are you hungry?" Claudia asked him, "Not really, had a big lunch, could use a glass of cold water." Craig responded. As she was getting his water Claudia noticed that Craig was pulling out a folder from his briefcase, she looks on curious but refrains from asking questions. With excitement Craig speaks, "So are you ready for your big day tomorrow? I know I can't wait to see you in action, I always love seeing you work." Claudia responds, "You know I'm not as nervous as I thought I would be, maybe tomorrow I will feel a little different. I'm anxious to see what kind of clientele I will be bringing in, that's what's exciting to me." As both of them continue to talk Craig is still fumbling with the folder he pulled out of his briefcase. As Claudia looks on she finally asks him, "What are you doing, you look a little lost with that folder, do you need help?" Craig laughs and responds, "Love sit down I have something that I feel is very important that I want to share with you, this is the next chapter in our lives." Claudia listens, "I know that everything seems to be moving fast with us, first I come back, then we re-conciliate, then our businesses are blooming but with all this positive energy flowing around us I still feel incomplete. I want us to be together for the rest of our lives and I was hoping that you felt the same way too, I never want to be away from you ever again." Claudia without hesitation responds, "Of course I feel the same way, I agree our lives have been at a fast pace but I've just learned to deal with it, what is it that your wanting to do to change Craig, get to the point." Craig continues, "I want us to move in together, I know you have this wonderful house that you purchased on your own but I want something for us, something that I was able to do, not just for me but for us." Claudia sat there speechless not knowing how to respond, Craig continues, "Look Love I'm not asking you to sell your house, I just want us to be together, I want to wake up with you, cuddle on a cold day, be a complete couple, I want to give you what you deserve and for the first time I can do that." Claudia still speechless finally responds, "There's nothing in this world that I would like more than to share the rest of my life with you, I don't know if I'm ready to let this house go but I am ready for the next step in our lives so I say let's go for it."

Craig couldn't believe his ears, he was so happy that he looked like the Nets just won the championship, Claudia was ecstatic herself, after the both of them settle down from there excitement Craig showed Claudia the prints to there new house. Craig begins to explain, "Now nothings set in stone, anything you want can be added or changed, even the location, I just want to feel us when you walk through those doors." Claudia looked on in amazement, "My God, this house is huge! Don't you think we should down size a bit? When am I going to have time to clean it?" Craig laughs, "That's why you have a house keeper Love." Claudia continues, "No I like cleaning my own house, if you don't mind let me sleep on it and together we can make changes." Craig responds, "Sounds good, you have no idea how happy I am Love, I promise you nothing but happiness."

As the both of them got ready for bed, it was a awkward moment. Since Craig came back, there wasn't an intimate moment shared. Either both of them worked late or both where to tired to even attempt so tonight was going to be special.

As Craig showered, Claudia lit candles all over the room. She sprayed the bed down with a soft scent and you could hear Luther playing softly in the back ground. She wore a black laced lingerie that she bought a long time ago that had never been worn. She was a little nervous because it had been so long. Claudia was a very romantic person and for once she wanted it her way, to her the ambiance was just right. As Craig made his way out of the shower he could smell the soft aroma burning in the room, he closed his eyes and took a whiff, "Um the room smells so good and feels so tranquil."

As he made his way to the bed Claudia stood over the foot board, "You startled me." Craig responds, "Sorry I didn't mean to scare you." Claudia responds back, Craig continues, "You look beautiful, are you going to join me?" As Craig spoke Claudia made her way to the bed, she slowly began to kiss him hugging him tight, Craig responds back in delight, as both of them begin to get lost in each others emotions Claudia realizes the song that's playing in the back ground, "If This World Were Mine by Luther" her body began to tingle all over, in her mind it added to a perfect evening and with that Claudia let herself go in her emotions and Craig had no idea that the song made her open her inhibitions to a night of love, lust, and sexual pleasures that both reached a peak of satisfaction and peaceful bliss. At the end of the night both of them lay-ed there in each others arms, happy, in love and at peace . . . .

As the sun rose up that morning, Craig had breakfast waiting for her. "There's nothing like a good morning breakfast to get your day started." Claudia responds, "Since when do you cook?" Craig with a laugh responds, "Hey I had to fend for myself plenty of times so I learned to manage, I hope you like it baby." As Claudia sat down to eat she began to think back to the first day they met. She never thought that they would be together again sharing there lives. Today was a big day for her and finally she had someone by her side to share her joy.

As they were getting ready to leave the phone rang, it was Claudia's mom. She called to wish Claudia luck with her new boutique, with everyone working it was hard for her to go, she was the one taking care of the kids, that's a grandma for you. She gave Claudia her blessings then the two of them where off.

Everyone from the office was already there to great Claudia, the excitement was starting to sink in. As Craig looked around his body filled with an abundance amount of pride, he was very proud of her. It was 9:00 in the morning and considering that it was early there was a huge group of people waiting for the big unveiling, Claudia was happy. Tony, as always, went beyond his call of duty, as a surprise for Claudia he had a special guest speaker to help unveil the boutique, Claudia had no idea what was going on. As Tony began to speak flashes started going, and you could hear everyone take a breath As the crowd turned to look the opposite direction, Claudia, confused, looked on as well. As they announced the guest speaker Claudia stood there speechless, it was Tamara, a famous plus size model that Claudia was dieing to have on one of her runway shows. Claudia was overwhelmed with excitement. As Tamara spoke about Claudia's line Claudia began to get flashbacks all the way to the beginning of her career, how she started and where she ended up at, it's been a long journey but well worth it. As Tamara wrapped up her speech it was time to cut the ribbon, at the count of three Claudia stood there proud, cameras flashing and finally the unveiling of the boutiques name. It was as simple as apple pie, the name of the boutique was "Claudia's".

As the day came to an end, Claudia was exhausted, everyone wanted to go to dinner but all Claudia wanted to do was go home and get into her comfort zone. Everyone understood so no one questioned her. As Craig drove up the driveway he looked over to Claudia, she was asleep in the passengers side. Craig parked the car and went over to help her out. My poor baby never a dull moment for you my love, he thought as he helped her out of the car.

As he helped her through the foyer Craig asked her "Are you hungry?" You could hear the tiredness in Claudia's voice as she spoke, "You know all I had was breakfast, and considering the long day I had I'm not really hungry. All I really want is my bed and pillow and I'll be happy." With that said Craig took off Claudia's shoes and helped her to her bed. As he tucked her in Claudia couldn't help but think how lucky she was to have someone as special as him in her life, at this point, she actually had forgotten the age difference between them but it didn't matter, age was nothing but a number.

Chapter 17

Two years have passed since Craig and Claudia's reconciliation, there new house was built not to far from Claudia's old one and business for the both of them was doing very well. Claudia kept busy between her fashion designs and boutique but Claudia's favorite place to be was the store, she loved interacting with the customers and the customers loved when she was there. Claudia didn't sell her house, instead she had her mother move in so she could be close to her. Holidays came and went as did birthdays and every time was a wonderful time for the both of them. They had there families together during the holidays and everyone seemed to get along, Claudia went from being alone to having family around all the time, she was loving it.

Craig had gone out of town on a business trip and Claudia started to notice that she was beginning to get tired more than usual. She hoped that her sickness wasn't taking it's toll on her again.

Every since her last episode everything seem to be OK so Claudia never told Craig about her condition, she just hoped that it would miraculously go away and she would never have to tell him. But as the days went by Claudia felt worst, it wasn't till one morning at the office when Claudia started to feel nauseous and faint, she excused herself from a meeting and barely made it to the bathroom to throw up. Lola followed her as quickly as she could. "Claudia, are you OK?" Claudia responds, "I think I ate something that didn't settle right with my stomach, I think I'll be OK." Lola responds with a laugh, "Ha, ha I bet your pregnant!" Claudia sat on the toilet with a weird look on her face, nooo she thought, pregnant?, but how? She was 44 years old, she doubted very seriously that she was pregnant. As she made her way out of the bathroom she responded to Lola, "Girl, your crazy! I'm not pregnant, I told you it's something I ate." Lola laughed again, "I was just kidding, but maybe you should get checked just in case your virus is acting up, you did tell Craig about it I'm assuming?" Claudia wiped her face then responded, "Actually, no, I haven't, I really have been doing good so I figured there was no reason to get him upset, besides as long as I follow Dr.'s orders I'm fine." Lola responds, "You should be ashamed of yourself! You were so mad when he wasn't honest with you and here you go, same thing different scenario. I think your wrong for not telling him." Claudia quickly responds, "Look I didn't ask for your opinion, if and when the time is right I'll tell him but as of now he doesn't need to know." Lola trying to keep it together responds back, "It's your life, I guess you know what your doing, just remember I told you so when it hits the fan." Claudia rushes out the bathroom talking through her teeth, "Why does she always have to be so sarcastic?, I didn't even ask for her help in the bathroom then I get lectured, I wish she would just mind her own business!" With that said Claudia went back to finish her meeting.

Before the day was over Claudia made an appointment with the doctor for first thing in the morning, Craig would be back in a couple of days and she wanted to fix whatever it was that might be broken, hopefully it was just one of those 24 hour stomach bugs and everything would be fine.

Claudia had a hard time sleeping that night, she couldn't help thinking about what Lola said, It wasn't fair for her to keep her sickness away from Craig. But what if it scares him away? What if he sees her as a burden, who wants to take care of an old lady with ailments? Sooner or later she would have to tell him but for now she decided that she would continue to keep it to herself.

The next day came and Claudia was a little nervous. She said a prayer that morning and hoped for the best. The doctor examined her and the last thing he asked from her was a urine specimen, the doctor had asked for it before so it didn't strike her as being odd, but he did ask her to wait so he could talk to her, that worried her. As she sat there in the waiting room the nurse finally called her back in to talk to the doctor, Claudia was so nervous. "Sit down Claudia, would you like a water?" Claudia anxious to hear what the doctor says responds, "No thank you Dr. can you please just get to the point of why you called me in here." The doctor calmly responds, "Well we got back your test and everything seems to be normal, except for one thing, it seems that in 7 months you are going to be a momma." Claudia sat there almost ready to faint, "A baby? Are you sure? I thought I couldn't have any children." The doctor responds, "Now why would you think that? Did anyone ever tell you that you couldn't?" Claudia, shocked, responds, "Well no, I just thought with my age that if I didn't have children by now I would never have any." "Well my dear obviously that's not true, but you are considered high risk for your age so I want to get you back in here so I can run test on you, just to make sure momma and baby are fine. Well congratulations, I wish you the best. Go talk to the front desk and they will set you up with some prenatal vitamins for meantime, until we get you situated. Do you have any questions?" Claudia sat there in disbelieve, "No doctor at this moment I'm speechless, I'm sure I'll have a whole list once I grasp what you have just told me." The doctor laughs, "Oh my dear, your gonna be just fine. I'll see you in two weeks, I'm going to leave you alone for a little while just close the door on your way out." Claudia sat there white as a ghost, she was going to have a baby, as the thought set in she began to cry, she was going to be a momma, everything was about to change.

Claudia called in to the office and had Tony handle things for the day. As she drove home she couldn't believe what was happening, she was going to be a mom. Feelings of excitement started to flow through her body, she couldn't wait to go and tell her mother. As she made her way to her old house, everything started to sink in, she really wanted to tell Craig first but since he was out of town she decided to wait till he got home so mom would be the first person she told. As she made her way in her mom was making lunch, "Ay Mija, come sit down and have some tuna with me," As Claudia made her way to the kitchen, the smell of the tuna made her sick! She excused herself and ran straight to the bathroom, as she made her way back to the kitchen her mother had a smile on her face. Before Claudia could say anything her mother already knew, "Your going to have a baby, right Mija?" "How did you know?" Claudia responds. Claudia's mom responds happy, "It's mothers intuition, I knew it when I saw you the other day, you had this glow and Craig couldn't seem to keep his eyes off you. That's how I knew." Claudia begins to cry, "Oh momma, I'm so happy but scared at the same time, I'm 44 years old! I shouldn't be having babies at this age, what about my condition? What if my body can't handle having a baby?" Claudia's mom responds, "God only gives you what you can handle, everything is going to be just fine, embrace the moment for what it is, your going to be a mom, that's the most precious gift god gives a woman, embrace it." With that said Claudia hugged her mom and cuddled with her like a baby, and within 7 months she will be doing the same . . . .

It was time for Craig to come back home and Claudia was ecstatic to see him, she couldn't wait to tell him the big news. She fixed her hair and makeup and put on a nice outfit for him, instead of going out to dinner she figured she would cook him a nice home cooked meal, something he always looked forward for especially after a business trip, she was excited. As he made his way to the door Claudia didn't wait for him to open it she swung it open before he could get the key in. "Wow, somebody missed me, I missed you too Love." Craig responds. Claudia gave him a big kiss, "It seemed like forever, how was your trip?" Craig ready for a hot shower responds, "It was OK, a lot of BS but we came to an agreement. Hey the table looks nice, are we having company?" Claudia responds, "No, just us two, I figured you were tired of all those business dinners out so I decided to cook you up something special." Craig responds, "Your so wonderful, what would I do without you?" "I'm sure you would manage" Claudia responds. Craig continues, "Let me go wash up and change then I'll be down for dinner, does that sound good to you." Claudia anxious responds, "Of course I'll have everything ready by the time you come down." With that said Craig went to change.

   Like Claudia said she had everything ready for him when he came down, as they sat down to eat Craig couldn't help but to stare at Claudia, "You look so beautiful, every time I see you, you take my breath away." Claudia begins to blush, "Stop it, your just saying that because your stuck with me for the rest of your life, so you have no choice but to be nice." Both of them begin to laugh, Craig continues the conversation, "So how did your days go? How was work?" Claudia responds, "Work was good, my days went by slow because you weren't here. I went and spend time with my mom so it was good." Craig continues, "Well that's good, you should be visiting your mom more often." Claudia continues to speak, "I haven't been feeling good lately so I decided to see the doctor . . . ." Craig interrupts, "The doctor? Is everything OK?" Claudia continues, "As a matter of fact there's something I need to tell you." Craig interrupts, "What's wrong?" Claudia continues anxiously, "Well . . . . it seems like . . . . in 7 months you are going to be a daddy!" Craig drops his fork, there's a long silence before he responds, "A daddy? You mean your going to have a baby?" Claudia looks at him amused, "Yes, that's what that means, your gonna be a daddy and I'm gonna be a momma." Craig jumps up from his chair spilling over his cup of water. "YES, YES, I'M GOING TO BE A FATHER!" Before you knew it Craig swept up Claudia spinning her in a circle, before he realizes what he's doing he responds, "Oh my God! I'm so sorry sit down my love, I hope I didn't hurt you or the little one?" Claudia responds laughing, "Is this what I have to put up with? I'm not going to break Love, I take it that your OK with this?" Craig responds, "Of course I am, why wouldn't I be? I'm going to be a Dad, a Dad, that's miraculous to me.

You have made me the happiest man in the world Claudia Cruse!" Claudia responds, "And you have made me the happiest woman, we are finally going to be complete!"

As the night settled in Craig and Claudia began to reminisce about the first time they met, laying on the sofa Craig is staring up to the ceiling, he begins to speak, "I never thought that we would make it this far, I mean I knew we would be together I just had a different vision of how our life would be. I always pictured us wining and dining in fine restaurants, you know things like that but here I am with the love of my life getting ready to start a family, amazing . . . ." Claudia responds, "So do you have regrets? Considering that's not the direction our life has taken." Craig sits up and responds, "Regrets? Of course not! This is better than my vision Love, I'm going to be a Dad! I love you so much and you have given me more than money could buy. So do I have regrets? The answer is definitely no and don't you ever think any different." Claudia took a deep breath, without any response she lay there thinking about her happiness, this is what she hoped for all her life, the age difference between them didn't exist anymore in her mind and she could care less what people would say, love made it's way home and it was time to enjoy the phase in there lives . . . .

Months passed and the pregnancy had really taken a toll on Claudia, she was in her 6th month but felt like she was ready to deliver any day. It was hard for her to make it to her boutique and Office like she used too, so she put Lola in charge of the boutique and Tony in charge of the office, it seemed to keep everyone happy and Claudia well rested. Craig had several business trips lined up so Claudia's mom would stay with her just in case anything happened. Craig had a problem leaving town at this point but Claudia reassured him that she would be just fine with her mother's love and care.

Everyone at the office seemed to be excited about the new arrival, what made it more exciting is the fact that neither Craig or Claudia wanted to know the sex of the baby, they wanted to do it the old fashion way and be surprised, so everyone at the office made bets for fun, loser would buy lunch. You could feel the positive energy flowing everywhere.

Craig was home early from his business trip and loved the fact that they could both be home. Claudia herself was happy because Craig had her spoiled, anything she wanted, she got. It was about 8:00 in the evening when they both started talking about baby names, if it was a boy Claudia wanted to name him after Craig and of course he agreed but they where both stuck on girl names, nothing appealed to them, "I guess if it's a girl we will know when we see her." Claudia speaks with calmness in her voice. As they both started to get ready for bed Craig turned to look at Claudia and noticed that she looked a little pail, "Are you OK my Love? You look like you don't feel good, do you want me to get you anything?" Claudia responds with her eyes closed, "You know Love I really don't feel well. I was thinking of going to visit the boutique tomorrow, but I don't know if I can. I feel weak, my head hurts, I feel Nassau all the time, all I want to do is sleep." Craig responds concerned, "Do you want me to call the doctor?" Claudia continues, "No I have a appointment coming up, I think I'll be OK if I rest. I don't have anything pending at the office or boutique so I think my team can handle it. If it's not to much to ask for please don't wake me up early, I'm going to try to sleep in as much as I can." Craig concerned about Claudia responds, "I'm going to call your mother tomorrow and ask her to come stay with you, I'm going to take ½ a day at the office so I'll be home around noon. I really don't want to leave you by yourself my Love, just in case." Claudia reassures Craig that it's not necessary for her mother to come over, "Love I just need to sleep and I'll be fine." Craig agrees and helps Claudia get ready for bed.

The months flew by fast, the time was almost near for there bundle of joy and Craig was ecstatic. Between the two families, and work between the both of them, there were gifts that covered everything for the baby, both Craig and Claudia were well ready for the happy arrival. Craig noticed that Claudia was very quiet, she usually was the life of the party but lately she really didn't say much and it worried him. "Love I'm so concerned about you, are you feeling alright?" Claudia interrupts, "I don't know if it's because I'm nervous, or the time is near, the doctor says everything has been coming out OK, but I still don't feel well, I'm ready to pop out this baby already." Craig couldn't help but laugh, "That bad huh? I'm so proud of you Love, your going to be a wonderful mother." Claudia smiled, "I hope so, I am ready for it, and I know you will be an excellent father too."

It was 5:00 in the morning and Craig woke up startled, at first he thought he was dreaming but as he began to wake up fully he could hear crying coming from the kitchen, it was Claudia. He jumped out of bed and raced to the kitchen, "What's the matter? Love what's wrong?!" Claudia could barely respond, "I don't know, I don't feel good, something's not right, I need to go to the hospital." With that said, Craig ran to get his shoes, he grabbed Claudia's night bag and tried to get her in the car as safe and as fast as he could, trying not to show that he was terrified.

As they pulled up to the emergency room Craig parked the car and ran to the other side to get Claudia out, she could barely respond to him so he got the attention of a paramedic that was getting ready to enter the hospital. "Mame, mame can you hear me, mame." Claudia could not respond. As he brought over a stretcher Craig's heart was pounding, he had never been through something like this before but he knew something was terribly wrong, as the paramedic wheeled her in Craig got on the phone to call her mother and his, all he wanted was for Claudia and the baby to be fine. The paramedic got the attention of a nurse, the nurse took her blood pressure and yelled, "Her blood pressure's low, we need to get her to ICU stat!" There seemed to be ciaos everywhere, Craig stood there lost, heart pounding, tears filling his eyes, all he could think about was Claudia and how much she wanted a family, how much he wanted one too, everything had to be fine.

Craig followed Claudia up to ICU, before he could see her he had to fill out paperwork, he could barely think, he just wanted to be with her. As he finished up his mother walked in with Claudia's, as he turned to see them he broke down, "I don't know what happened, she said she didn't feel well last night but she looked OK, how can I not know that she was feeling that bad? I feel like a horrible person to not see the signs!!" As he kept on, and on, Claudia's mom, in a calm voice, interrupted, "Craig, you need to calm down and get it together, my daughter needs you now. We know it's not your fault, there's no way that you could of known that she was this sick, so calm down so you can go see her and be with her." Craig's mom responds, "Son, she's right, you need to get it together, you know Claudia would not like to see you like this, take a deep breath, she's going to be OK, save your energy because when that baby get's here your gonna need it." Craig calms down and smiles, "Thank you both, don't know what I would do without my family, OK, I'm calm, I'm going to go see her now."

As Craig walked in to see Claudia his heart broke, they had her hooked up to a IV and a oxygen mask to help her breath, Craig had never seen Claudia so weak, she was always busy, no time for rest, so this was hard for him to see. As he sat down next to her he whispered to her, "Love, I'm here, if you needed a little extra attention all you had to do was ask, no need for all this drama now." Claudia squeezed his hand to let him know she heard him. Craig continued, "This is not the way I was planning to ask you, I was going to wait till the baby was born, I was thinking when all this is done would you do me the honors of marrying me, I know you can't answer me now, just sleep on it." Before Craig could continue you could hear a very faint voice coming from Claudia, "Love, I . . . . marry . . . . you . . ." Craig's eyes began to water, "I'm hopping that's a yes?" Claudia nodded faintly. As Craig sat there, holding Claudia's hand the nurse walked in, "Are you the husband?" Craig responded, "Yes I am, well not yet, but yes." The nurse continued, "OK I'm taking that as a yes, your wife, is having complications, when you brought her in her blood pressure was very low, the virus seemed to have kicked in again making . . ." Craig with a startled look on his face interrupts, "Virus, what virus?" The nurse continues, "Your wife didn't tell you? Ms. Cruse has been dealing with a bacterial infection for years now and for some reason the doctors can not pin point where it is coming from or what is causing it, so from time to time she has weak spells that causes her body to almost completely shut down, making it hard for her everyday routine, because of her age and pregnancy it has taken a toll on her body, so right now the doctors are trying to keep her stable so she can deliver the baby." Craig stood there shocked! This was the first time he had ever heard of her infection, and he was speechless. As he tried to get his compulsion together he begins to speak, "So what does this mean for her and the baby? Is she going to be OK?" The nurse responds, "Sir, I wish I had a answer for you, we are just going to have to wait and see. The doctor is getting ready to run her body with a antibiotic hopefully she takes to it and everything will be OK, as soon as we get her stable the doctor is going to induce labor, we have to just wait and see. If you need anything my name is Amy, just call on me and I will be more than happy to help you. Don't worry she's in good hands." As the nurse stepped out Craig couldn't help but walk out behind her, as he made his way to the waiting room he began to cry, how could she not tell him? This was not the time to be upset over it, he was just trying to understand.

Craig walked into the waiting room and Lola, Tony and his wife, and a few of Claudia's workers were there waiting, Claudia's mom could see the worry in his face, "Craig, is everything OK?" Craig sat there with his hands over his face, silence for a while, he responds, "With all do respect Ms. Cruse, If I come off as being upset at you I'm not it's just the situation, but why didn't Claudia tell me that she was sick? If I had known I could of helped her." Before Claudia's mom could respond, Lola interacts, "Craig, right now is not the time to ask why, Claudia had her reasons, why I don't know but she did. You have to respect that and move on, let's worry about getting the baby here and her better, OK?" Craig takes a deep breath, "I know, I know, but I'm just trying to understand all this. But your right, I need to focus on my family getting better." Lola sighs, and in her mind she thinks, I'm gonna strangle that girl for not tell him. Everyone starts to calm down when the nurse rushes in to get Craig.

Craig runs up to the nurse with everyone following him, "Mr. Sanches, Claudia's not responding to the antibiotic so we are going to have to do an emergency C-section to get the baby out, as soon as I have news, I'll come get you, try to be calm OK, the doctor is doing everything he can." Craigs heart feels so heavy, how can all this be happening, it's suppose to be a joyful moment, all that ran through his mind was Claudia. One hour had passed and still no news, Craig sat in the corner hoping no one would come talk to him but someone always did, everyone just wanted to show him that they cared. Lola walked over to where he was at and sat down next to him, "You holding up OK?" Craig looks at her lost, "Not really, I just want my girl and my baby, I want to be able to hold them both in my house on my sofa! Is that to much to ask for, because I didn't think it was!" Lola calmly responds, "I know it's hard Craig, it's hard for all of us, but you need to just have faith, Claudia said that's what you always say, have faith, so it's time to take your own advice and put it in God's hands. The doctor should be coming in soon." Before they could finish there conversation the doctor came in, "Family here for Claudia Cruse? Craig stood up quick, "Yes that's me." The doctor continues, "Well we have her stable but as of right now it's very critical, she's in a coma and all we have to do now is wait. The baby is just fine, she weighed 8 lbs 2 ounces . . . ." Craig interrupts, "You said she, did we have a girl?" The doctor continues, "Oh yes, I'm sorry, it's a girl, a healthy baby girl. After we get Ms. Cruse settled I'll let you come in to see her, but only two at a time." Craig worn out responds, "Thank you doctor." Craig turned around to look at everyone, "It's a girl" Everyone begins to clap and yell except for Claudia's mom, she walks up to Craig, "What's wrong with Claudia?" Craig looks at Claudia's mom with sadness in his eyes then responds, "They have her stable but she's in a coma, they are going to call us back when they have her settled in. Claudia's mom begins to cry, Craig hugs her speechless, he has no more words to say, all they can do now is wait . . . .

Everyone from the office decided to leave and give Craig and the family space, Lola decided to stay besides she was family. As the day began to wind down the nurse finally came down to take them back to see Claudia, Craigs heart was pounding. Craig decided to let Claudia's mom go in first, Lola went with her. As Craig sat back and waited, he began to think back to when they first met. She was different all right, he would of never thought that anyone like her would love him as much as she did, he felt blessed. He also began to think about there age, he had actually forgotten the distance between them, you couldn't tell with Claudia's personality, that's what kept her looking young he thought. He laughed with thoughts on how she would pick on him when he couldn't keep up with her, "Who's the young one here?" She would boast. As his mind began to wonder he dozed off.

Thirty minutes had passed and Craig woke to shaking, it was Claudia's mom trying to wake him up, "Craig, Craig, you can go see her now." Craig got up startled, Claudia's mom continued, "I'm going to go home with Lola, she is going to stay with me the night, if anything happens please call us, I don't want to leave but I'm no good to you if I don't rest a little." Craig responds, "No, no, I understand, I promise I'll call you as soon as I hear something, thank you for everything." Craig give's Claudia's mom a hug and she hugs him back. As Craig made his way to the room he reminded himself to keep it together, he didn't know what to expect. As he walked in it looked like Claudia was in a peaceful sleep and Craig felt a little more comfortable seeing her that way. As he sat down next to her he whispered like he did the first time to her, "I'm here Love, I don't know if you know it or not but we had a girl, I haven't seen her yet because I'm waiting on you, so the sooner you wake from your beauty nap the sooner we can see her together." Tears filled Craig's eyes as he spoke to her.

Craig stayed with Claudia all night long and into the early morning before a nurse came to wake him, "Mr. Sanches, Mr. Sanches?" Craig awoke, "Can you step out a moment so we can change her up, I'll call you when we are done." Craig nodded. As he walked out into the lobby he decided to go down and grab a cup of coffee, he didn't drink coffee but needed something to wake him up. As he made his way back to the room the nurse had just finished up, "she's all nice and fresh Mr. Sanches." Craig responds angrily, "Nice and fresh, she's not some kind of flower arrangement, or air spray, she's my wife! Can you please have a little more respect for her than that?!" The nurse's eyes began to water, "I'm sorry . . . . I didn't mean it that way, I just meant that she was cleaned up and made comfortable that's all, I really didn't mean anything bad by it, I'm sorry." Craig felt bad for going off like that, it wasn't her fault, he apologized and sat next to her again.

The time came and went like it had been, he turned the TV on but nothing caught his attention. Claudia's mom and Lola came in and spent hours with her, Lola read fashion magazines to her, and Claudia's mom fixed her hair, as everyone left Craig was relieved he just wanted to be alone with Claudia. It was finally calm and Craig began to talk to Claudia, "Oh Love how I miss talking to you, and hearing your voice, I wish you would wake up, I haven't seen our daughter because I'm waiting for you, please wake up I need you, I miss you." As tears ran down his face Claudia's eyes opened, Craig looked at her with a sense of relief, "You woke up my Love, I knew you would." Before he could finish she tried to speak, "I'm not . . . . going to make it . . . . I'm to tired . . . ." Craig couldn't believe what he was hearing, he thought maybe he was hearing her say the wrong thing. "Love, no your awake, your going to be fine, Love, can you hear me?" Claudia tries to respond, "I . . . . love you . . . . take . . . . our baby . . . . tired." Craig couldn't believe his ears, he was not ready to let her go, he couldn't, what was he going to do without her! As she closed her eyes again Craig ran out to get a nurse, "Can you get a chaplain in here as fast as you can I think I'm losing my girl!" Craig was frantic, and lost, but he tried to hold on as much as he could, the nurse's came in to check on Claudia, "Sweetheart I think you need to call your family, she's going fast." Craig was completely lost, he called her mother and told her to rush over, as he hung up the phone the chaplain arrived. Craig could barely speak, "I know this is out of the ordinary and I know it probably isn't legit but could you please go over marriage vows for us, we were suppose to get married after the baby was born and this would mean so much to us, please I'm begging." The chaplain looked at Craig speechless but honored his wishes.

As the chaplain stood there reading there vows, Claudia would open her eyes and then closed them, Craig felt her energy in the room, as they finished up there vows Claudia's mom stood in the back and listened crying, Craig crying also. As the chaplain blessed them both he gave Claudia her last rites and left the room. There was a sense of calmness after he left, Lola and Tony showed up as did Craig's mom, Craig stood on one side of the bed and her mother on the other. As the time passed, Claudia slowly started to fade away, Lola and Tony couldn't take it so they left the room. Claudia's mom held on to her as long as she could, then she couldn't anymore, Craig's mom comforted her. Craig held on to her hand tight, Claudia started to take her final breath, Craig crying uncontrollably, "I love you my Love, thank you for giving me such a precious gift, I always will remind her of you, and what you went through to have her, I love you . . . ." And with that Claudia passed away.

Craig sat there in silence and peace filled the air, her mom left the room to make phone calls and Craig's mom left to be with her. It was hard for him to grasp the thought that she was gone. As he sat there still, motionless, a nurse walks into the room, "Mr. Sanches" he responds, "Yes?" the nurse continues handing him a note, "This is for you, I met Claudia a couple of months ago. She started to feel bad and came for weekly visits the doctor's had her infection under control but she might of felt something was not right because she wrote this letter and ask me to give it to you, if need be. I'm sorry to have to do this, she became one of my friends, but I promised her that I would if I had to. I'm so sorry for your loss but this letter meant a lot to her, so here you go, again, I'm sorry." Craig took the letter but had nothing to say. He continued to sit there motionless till finally the morgue came to pick her up, she was gone.

As he made his way to the waiting room there was a chair in the corner by the window so he decided to sit there, as he sat he decided to read the letter:

My dearest Love, if you are reading this letter then sadly I have parted this earth. Don't be sad my Love because one day we will be together again. I'm sorry for not telling you I was sick but I felt it was better that way. You are the love of my life and I will be watching you

151

from up above. We had one dilemma before I parted
and that was a name for our little girl, I knew all along
that it was a girl, mothers intuition, when I met you, you
always told me that faith brought us together, or have
faith, so I thought it would be appropriate if we would
name our daughter just that, Faith, because you believed
we were able to find our way back to each other and
conceive this beautiful gift of life and love. Have no worries
because you will be able to do what you always wanted to
do, give her everything she needs and wants, you'll be
a wonderful father, I have to go now, I love you always

Your Wife, Claudia

Craig, for the first time, felt peace in his heart, it was time for him
to meet his daughter. As he stood there the nurse made her way over
to him with the baby, "I want you to meet someone who's wanting
to meet there daddy." She handed the baby over to him. Craig looked
at her for the first time, she looked just like Claudia, "Hey baby, I'm
your daddy, guess what mommy left, a beautiful name for you, yes
she did, we are going to have to introduce you to everyone as Faith,
Faith Sanches, I have so much to tell you about your mommy." He
kissed her on the forehead and held her gently, as he looked out the
window it began to rain, then thoughts of the first date they had ran
through his mind, he remembered Claudia and how she said the rain
felt like candy kisses as it fell from the sky, so Craig knew she made
it to heaven and she was throwing candy kisses down to them . . . .